SYNCHRONICITY

an Interstellar Fantasy Thriller

Episode One

Anza Qi

and the

Chronicle of Unchangeable Changes

Copyright © 2013-2016 by William Nona -0TXU001907630

Library of Congress Control Number: 1-1351400371

ISBN-13: 978-0692570944 - Nona Publishing
ISBN-10: 0692570942

Registered with The Writers Guild of America, west, Inc.

This is a work of fiction. Names, characters, places and incidents either are the product of the author's imagination or are used fictitiously, and any resemblance to any actual persons, living or dead, events, or locales is entirely coincidental. However, reference to the duplicate planet Theia, and the four-dimensional planet of Anon represent real places.

This book was printed in the United States of America.

Prologue

Long before the events of this story, Daiyu, the Black Jade, attempted to take control of the Sun Star parallel planets Earth and Theia. Nous, the cosmic voice responsible for planetary balance, defeated Daiyu casting him out of his four-dimensional world to the Space-Between Dimensions.

The secrets to planetary balance are locked in the Chronicle of Unchangeable Changes on Earth, and only accessible through the Tome of Legends on Theia using the Sacred Oglala Crest cipher. Subsequently, Nous switched the Tome and Chronicle leaving the cipher on Theia to thwart the use of its magic where it remained for millenniums until an unbalance occurred making the Sacred Oglala Crest vulnerable to claim by anyone.

Access to the all-powerful Chronicle of Unchangeable Changes has been handed-down to the Chosen-One throughout the ages to safeguard the equilibrium of the synchronistic planets.

Anza Qi, a thirteen-year-old Chinese-American boy on Earth will soon learn that it is his destiny to be the custodian of the ancient secrets.

* * * * * * *

It is morning, the temperature outside our Starcruiser Totfote is about 2.7 Kelvin, and pitch dark as our inter-planetary travel takes us from Alpha Centauri toward the Sun Star. Planet Theia is seen chasing Planet Earth, collides and both planets spin-off a Moon. Theia bounces back taking place as Earth's identical parallel planet on the opposite side of the Sun. All the planets in the solar system spin faster and faster indicating the passing of millenniums.

Our Starcruiser experiences a potholed ride as it passes through a Coronal Loop and catches a Solar Wind, which catapults us toward Planet Theia. Totfote kicks into hyper-drive with a bang, rocketing past the Sun in a Space-Time Continuum as the spinning planets are slowing down. As we get closer, we see an image of another planet, a fourth dimensional planet that fades and disappears as we pass.

From our seats just behind the pilot and navigator, we see the ground whiz by as Totfote dematerializes leaving our presence on Theia. As Interlopers we can observe, sometimes be heard, but we can never be seen.

Two identical planets on the opposite side of the Sun with almost identical and synchronistic occupants and happenings is an unusually strange phenomenon, but a fourth dimensional planet with composite synchronistic places and occupants is an anomaly that causes one to think our Universe is a lot more than meets the eye.

The equilibrium child Nous, (an Epicene) moves in and out of the parallel worlds ever aware of planetary balance, lives on the World of Anon. The Interstitial World of Anon is a four-dimensional resultant aberration of the lost days of February 29th and 30th combined from the Earth-Theia calendar, and a collection of all composite inhabitants from both planets.

The Worlds appear to be 100 years apart, but are always in the present time, which makes it logical to transport something or someone to the other planet without disrupting the *past or future*. This trans-dimensional travel phenomenon was created near the beginning ... shortly after the 'spin-off'. Theia spun backwards; 100 years behind Earth in development.

However, this does not preclude the *imbalance* that occurs when any person or object transports between parallel planets. Any dissimilarity must be corrected by the return of the person or object, or its counterpart, before the next February 29th or the planets will be destroyed. Interlopers and their spacecraft must also leave or face destruction, unless they undergo the RSR (Replication Synchronization Ritual).

The equilibrium child's interplanetary travel does not affect planetary balance.

We are drawn to a happening in a Theia countryside.

Chapter One

The Happening

It's a very cold winter day in Twentieth Century Mid-western U. S. A. countryside on the Planet Theia as the horse-wrangler-looking stable boy Dimitri Talbot returns to the Softwind Farm stable riding the prize thoroughbred stallion, 'Runs like the Wind'.

Emera Softwind, a remarkably young looking 50's Lakota Indian Grandfather is walking into the stable with his traditional cane, wearing blue jeans, a multi-colored flannel shirt and moccasins, as Dimitri dismounts. He witnesses the stableboy stuffing a crest into the pocket of his jeans.

"What are you doing?" he asks.

"Nothing sir," he responds.

"I saw you take the crest from the saddle. You know it's a Sacred Oglala Crest from Golden Elk (Lakota Medicine Man and Shape Shifter), and must remain with the saddle while it is transported to the White Buffalo Calf Woman festival."

"You crazy old man, I took nothing."

"You put it in your pocket. Now give it here, and we'll be done with it," he demands.

"I took nothing that isn't mine."

Dimitri turns and runs out of the stable laughing.

Emera raises his cane and shouts, "Come back here or I'll put a curse on you. I'll change you into a bird, an appalling raven," he commands raising his cane higher.

The tall and lanky Dimitri stops; his long sandy hair settles on his shoulders as he takes off his cowboy hat. He turns and walks slowly to the stable pushing past Emera, "I can put on curses too; so be careful."

"You cannot."

"I will turn this horse into a statue, and send him to the other world."

"What do you know of the other world?"

"I know about the Tome of Legends and the magic of the Sacred Oglala Crest."

"NO!" Shouting, "That's impossible. You're lying;" he looks puzzled, "the Tome is in the other ---"

"The other world," Dimitri's face tightens as he lies, "I have been to the other world."

The powerfully built Emera grabs his arm and turns him around with a quick move. "Give me the Crest."

Dimitri pulls away and starts to run out of the stable.

Emera, with a determined look, raises his cane. A breeze comes up and unfurls a Tribal Waluta attached to the top of the Vision Quest Cane. He begins chanting 'Great Spirit, take away this bad boy, send him to Earth' in his Lakota tongue, "Wakatanka, aye, aya sica hoksila, aya sica hoksils icu Makoce," louder and louder, over and over until a small twister forms, and locks-in on Dimitri stopping him in his tracks.

Dimitri grabs the horse and shouts 'change to a statue' in Lakota, "Yuto keca kakapi," as the horse morphs into a bronze statue.

The twister scoops up the bronze statue and Dimitri, the Raven, sending them into space with a sonic boom.

As the Raven and horse start to go up into space Dimitri cries, "You crazy old man, you're starting a ...," his words fade.

In the shadows of the stable, the foreman Nicholas Gray Wolf is quietly watching the happening.

Emera's grandson, Xandr Softwind, and his cousin Yellow Flower are on horseback in an adjacent meadow; Xandr is wearing traditional Lakota leather shirt, blue jeans and moccasins while Yellow Flower is in a typical beaded wool dress and skin boots. They feel the shockwave, and race to the Softwind Farm.

The curious thirteen-year-olds dismount quickly and run into the stable.

Xandr, a handsome soft-spoken full-blooded Lakota boy hugs his grandfather as Yellow Flower stands by quietly. "What happened, are you okay, Lala?" asks the boy.

"I'm just fine. It's that terrible stable boy."

"What did he do? Where is he?"

*   *   *   *   *   *   *

Daiyu, the Black Jade, is watching the happening in his Cosmos Comprehender while Katipo, a slender shapely female with silky-black waist length hair, in a black form-fitting outfit with a Latrodectus emblem on her chest and wearing Latrodectus Bracelets, stands at his side. Daiyu is an overwhelming figure more than seven feet tall with a soft and inviting smile on his classic face. Weird as it may seem he instantly changes appearance with his moods and becomes a ghostly malicious entity with great powers that can destroy with hand-launched thunderbolts as fast as light speed.

Katipo was born of Chinese-Lakota ancestry in a forbidden interaction between occupants of the parallel planets who met on the four-dimensional world Eartheia. Her parents of high political stature traveled from Earth and Theia respectively to attend a yearlong Interplanetary Leadership Council. Her parents had to return to their respective planets when the conference was completed; Katipo remained on Eartheia, because to live on either planet without a counterpart would cause an imbalance.

Eartheia was inhabited by wayward Karmic beings from both planets serving as keepers of the Karmic causality records and Council Chambers. Anon reinstated these beings as composite Ea'ians, which populated the planet He renamed after Himself.

At the time of Katipo's birth Daiyu, with restored karma, was in good favor with the Immortal Unknown and raised her as his daughter on Anon with his human wife Wachiwi. After Wachiwi passed, Daiyu reverted to the way of the Zgach and was exiled once more to the Space-Between taking the child Katipo with him.

Born in the fourth dimension allows Katipo 'limited-time visits' to either planet without causing imbalance.

RSR is not allowed for Space-Between Dimensions or four-dimensional inhabitants.

* * * * * * *

The Black Jade throws a Thunderbolt at the raven and statue changing them into fluid forms.

"The sacred crest is mine for the taking," he says turning his head away with a sinister smile as he commands Katipo. "You will go to Earth and retrieve it."

* * * * * * *

We, the invisible interlopers, are amazed.

Solo, our pilot asks, "What just happened?"

As his Universal Portal Prompter materializes, Duo, the navigator, replies, "Let's see," Duo's fingers move like a flash over the futuristic keypad. The screen is scanning through a variety of images and captures a three-dimensional event of a raven and the bronze statue of a horse traveling in space; multi-snapping at the screen in an attempt to jump out of the Prompter.

The trans-dimensional happening is destined for the Twenty-first Century mid-western U. S. A. Planet Earth.

With a brilliant flash of light and thunderous clap, the fluid bronze statue of the horse, 'Runs like the Wind', and the raven pass through the roof of an abandoned barn on the Qi Farm.

Our Starcruiser materializes. Suddenly without a word from our pilot or navigator the Universal Portal Prompter expands, sucking us into it with a zap, we are auto-secured in the quasi-invisible XR trans-tension restraint system and we find ourselves traveling through a space-time continuum arriving on Planet Earth simultaneously with the raven and bronze horse. Totfote dematerializes as it did before, the XR restraints release, but this time we become semi-fluid beings that can move through walls to observe the happenings without being noticed, leaving us disorientated and wondering what is going to happen next.

The fluid statue materializes as it lands in the center of the room with a thunderous clap and a brilliant flash of light. The raven is close behind landing in the rafters.

* * * * * * *

In an adjacent meadow, a synchronistic winter day on the Planet Earth, thirteen-year-old Anza Qi and his cousin Qingling, also thirteen are riding their horses and hear the deafening sound.

Anza, an expert rider who appears to be awkward in his baggy pants and sneakers makes a sharp turn to Qingling summoning her to follow with a simple follow-me movement of his head as he jambs his heels into the horse's side. Qingling responds without a word and they race to the Qi Farm stopping in a cloud of dust. Anza wants to be cool and always wears red frame Aviator glasses.

Anza's grandfather, Phir Qi, a tall youthful and noble looking man with a moustache and goatee matching his silky shoulder-length black hair, which seems to meld into the collar of his black leather jacket, witnessed the thunder and flash and rushes from the farmhouse getting to the old barn as the teens dismount.

Phir towers over his diminutive grandson rustling the boy's short curly layback hair, with his hand, in a gentle it'll-be-okay-fashion as they walk slowly and cautiously into the barn. They stop when they see the bronze statue. Phir intuitively knows the statue came from Theia, and it is going to be trouble.

Anza, Qingling, and Phir Qi are synchronistic duplicates of Xandr Softwind, Yellow Flower and Emera Softwind, but of Chinese descent.

"What's happening Yeye?" The timid Anza asks with the endearing Chinese word for grandfather.

"It has happened; the worst."

Qingling shouts with an impatient tone, "The worst what? What's going on?"

Anza removes his sunglasses for a brief moment displaying surprise in his big brown eyes and says, "That statue wasn't here before," turning back with a quick glance at Phir he puts the shades back on and asks, "where'd it come from?"

Solo speaks, "How'd we get here?"

Duo speaks with a finger to his lips, "Quiet, they might hear."

Qingling looks around, and asks, "Who said that?"

Phir Qi looks around with a quizzical frown and whispers to Anza, "We've got some interlopers."

Anza looks around uncertain as to what he is looking for and shrugs his shoulders, "Inter what?"

Phir searches the barn with suspicious eyes spotting the raven perched in the rafters, "This is not good. Come along," he turns and leaves the barn with the kids obediently behind. They go into the country style kitchen, "There are homemade cookies on the counter, anybody hungry?"

The petite Qingling tosses her pink-banded straw cowgirl hat onto the seat of a kitchen chair revealing her waist length pigtail black hair with bangs as she darts to the refrigerator, "I'll get the milk."

Phir unconsciously stares out the kitchen window at the old barn. A concerned look fills his ageless Chinese face as he realizes the time has come to pass his legacy on to Anza, and educate him in the way of the Chronicle of Unchangeable Changes.

He turns to the kids sitting at the table and looks at Qingling, "You should get on home. Your parents will be worried. I'll have Nigel bring your horse around," he talks into his cell phone, "Bring Q's horse around."

Qingling looks up, "Okay, but?"

"No buts, off with you."

Phir is quick to command his grandson as Anza and Qingling start to run out, "Sūnzi! He raises his voice a little, "I want you to stay."

The kids hug, and Qingling runs out, mounts her horse and rides away.

Phir sits staring down at the table as Anza quietly washes the dishes setting them aside to dry; knowing not to ask any questions. He hangs his towel and looks at his grandfather with curious eyes.

Phir looks at Anza and whispers, "Come with me, It's time. First, go and get the silver box from my room. It's in the top drawer on the right."

Anza runs off, and returns with the silver box. Phir takes his arm, and leads him to the Grand Room filled with ancient Chinese treasures. They stop facing a paneled wall.

Phir waves his hands and arms as he incants 'open portal' in Chinese, "Dakai ménhu," the wall becomes transparent and a room appears behind the wall. Phir takes Anza's hand, "Come Sūnzi."

Anza is squeamish and frightfully resists as Phir leads him through the wall into the obscured room.

"What is this place?"

"It is the Chamber Obscura, a very secret place."

* * * * * * *

The Raven peers through a window on the far side of the Grand Room as Anza and Phir disappear into the Chamber Obscura.

There is a large white leather-bound book resting on an elegant antique crystal glass podium in the center of the room. The walls are covered with ancient Chinese scrolls, paintings of mystical spiritual-like beings and maps of solar systems. The floor looks like water, and the ceiling seems to be a million miles away with stars everywhere.

A slight gesture from Phir and an ancient oval Yin Yang incense burner sitting on a tall slender table fires up and emits a misty blend of lavender and sage aroma adding a cleansing serenity to the room.

Anza looks around, breathes-in the incense aroma and focuses on the book, "The Tome of Legends?"

Phir Qi nods with a small smile, "Take the ring from the box, and put it on the first finger of your right hand with the diamond towards your finger tip."

The nervous Anza takes the ring and places it on the first finger of his left hand, "What do I do now?"

Phir looks softly at his grandson, knowing the burden he must pass on to him, "The ring *must be* on the right hand, then point to the Tome of Legends," he emphasizes, "things will happen that you will not understand. You must trust me, and do as I ask."

Anza takes the Magical Transfer Ring, which has an oval faceted Tanzanite stone surrounded by ancient writings and a small diamond, puts it on the first finger of his right hand and points at the Tome of Legends.

The diamond sparkles sending a Purple colored laser-like beam to the white book. The beam emits ethereally harmonious sounds as if the angels were performing a symphony.

The Tome begins to glow as the pages start turning. Anza quickly pulls his hand back in fear. The pages stop turning. He looks up at Phir.

"Don't be afraid Sūnzi. Point!"

"But, what?"

Phir looks at his grandson lovingly, but with authority.

"Okay, okay."

Anza points. The glowing pages start turning again. Phir takes a deep breath and goes into a trance.

The silence of the Chamber Obscura is broken as the voice of Emera Softwind speaks from Planet Theia, "I am here. You have seen the raven and the statue?"

Anza pulls his hand back. The glow fades; Phir still in the trance, gestures and Anza points again.

The Tome of Legends glows again, and Phir speaks, "How did this calamity happen?"

* * * * * * *

As Anza, Qingling, and Phir Qi on Planet Earth experience the interplanetary transference, so do their counterparts on Planet Theia.

Totfote materializes and we instinctively climb aboard for our trip to the Planet Theia. Solo leads the way and we sit in an open cabin directly behind the pilot and navigator, and are auto-secured in the quasi-invisible XR transtension restraint system.

Solo instructs, "Let's go."

Duo commands with authority, "Data 84342," and his Universal Portal Prompter materializes. His fingers seem to fly across the futuristic keypad. Totfote transforms into a transparent cylindrical spacecraft; we are secured and ready to go.

Duo strikes an illuminated pad as the Universal Portal Prompter isolates a glowing image of Theia, "Fold spacetime."

Solo strikes another pad at the command center, and suddenly with a soul wrenching blast the Portal Prompter expands sucking *us* into it, and *we* find ourselves trans-traveling through a space-time continuum arriving at the Softwind Farm on Planet Theia.

Our Starcruiser hovers and slowly lowers to the ground. The XR restraints release and we instinctively stand as Tot-fote dematerializes leaving us in a fluid state on Planet Theia. We seem to glide into and through the house stopping next to Xandr and Emera.

Xandr and Emera Softwind are standing in their Chamber Obscura on Theia. Emera places a colorful Lakota ceremonial shawl over Xandr's slender shoulders. The walls are covered with Lakota Indian scrolls and paintings of mystical spiritual-like beings and maps of solar systems. The floor looks like water, and the ceiling seems to be a million miles away with stars everywhere.

Emera Softwind gestures and a small flame appears under a smudge bowl floating above a tree trunk in the corner of the room and containing a blend of a cedar and sweetgrass. A classic Lakota healing aromatic scent fills the room.

Except for the wooden podium, tree trunk, aroma and the Lakota Indian images, the room is just like the Chamber Obscura on Planet Earth.

Xandr is wearing his Magical Transfer Ring on the first finger of his left hand and has a Carved Wood Box under his arm. The ring has an oval Alexandrite stone surrounded by ancient writings and a small diamond that is emitting an ever-changing bluish-green colored beam to the Chronicle.

They watch the Chronicle of Unchangeable Changes, which rests on a Podium carved from a tree trunk; vibrate with a mysterious glow and turning pages. A red burning void near the top of the podium seems to be groaning with pain like a buffalo, which has lost its mate to an arrow. The Sacred Oglala Crest is missing.

Emera is in a trance speaking to Phir Qi, "... it is the stable boy. I changed him into a raven and sent him to Earth, but he has taken the horse and the Sacred Oglala Crest with him," he breathes a big sigh, "as a raven he cannot control the powers of the Crest, but he can interact with his alter ego, and take other life forms."

We hear Phir Qi question Emera Softwind, "Why was the Crest with the saddle? It belongs in the podium under the Chronicle of Unchangeable Changes."

"It was released from the podium so the stone in its center could be joined with the Sacred Calf Pipe at the celebration of the White Buffalo Calf Woman. The white saddle on 'Runs like the Wind' was the instrument of cartage, but now there is an ache in the podium."

"It is the secret key to the magic of the Tome of Legends here on Earth, and must be returned."

* * * * * * *

Totfote materializes and we climb aboard for a trip to the Planet Earth. Solo leads the way directing us to our seats in the open cabin directly behind the pilot and navigator. We sit and are auto-secured in the quasi-invisible XR trans-tension restraint system.

Solo instructs, "Let's go."

Duo commands with authority, "Data 32784," and his Universal Portal Prompter materializes. His fingers flash across the futuristic keypad. Totfote transforms once again for the trip to the other side of the Sun Star.

Solo strikes another pad at the command center, and suddenly with the typical soul wrenching blast the Portal expands sucking us in; we find ourselves traveling again through a space-time continuum.

We arrive at our destination and instinctively stand up as XR releases and Totfote dematerializes leaving us near the old barn on the Planet Earth. As Interlopers, we are free to move about the Qi Farm in our fluid state for a limited time without going through the Replication Synchronization Ritual.

* * * * * * *

The Raven leaves his position at the window and flies right over our heads into the old barn landing on the statue's saddle.

The bird looks around, pulls the crest from under his feathers and flies off to a distant cave. Searching for a safe place, he finds a crevice high up in a dark place and hides the Crest. He flies down to a small pool, and sits on a rock looking into the water. His reflection appears and slowly changes into an apparition of Dimitri Talbot.

The reflection speaks, "We have to get the Tome of Legends from the boy."

The Raven responds, "We? I am you, and you are me. I'm a raven and, and you're no help."

"You have a helper," he points, "there, meet Natso."

A raccoon appears from behind a rock.

"Natso? A raccoon, a raccoon?" he squawks, "A raccoon called Natso. You gotta be kidding; me and a raccoon? What was he before ... before becoming a raccoon? How can he help?"

Notso positions itself like a bull ready for the charge, pawing the ground. He morphs into a huge ten-foot-tall Gnashing Teeth Black Raccoon Monster.

"Wow!" Exclaims the Raven as he flies off.

* * * * * * *

Phir Qi looks at Anza as they finish their episode with Emera and Xandr. He sees the wonder and confusion on his face, "Come with me Sūnzi, I want to show you something,"

"More secret rooms?"

"We are going to a place where you will understand. Come with me."

Anza puts his shades on as they leave the Chamber Obscura; they go out of the house and walk along a path in the meadow. The path changes from dirt to a seemingly endless green carpet with one cedar tree by its side that moves as they walk, remaining in the middle of the path's entire visible length.

"Yeye? Where are we? I've never been here before."

"Ah, but you have Sūnzi. I brought you here when you were very small."

"But, I can see our house. How is ---?"

Phir interrupts his grandson, "It's a place you can come when you have special things to do, and you don't understand."

"What kinds of things, what is this place?"

"It's called the Path of Knowledge."

"Can anybody else see it? Okay ... Okay! So-o-o ... where does it go? Why are we here? Why haven't I seen it before? I've walked ---"

"Sūnzi, Sūnzi. So many questions," Phir takes Anza's arm, "come along. It hasn't been the right time ... until now.

But, now, now we are here, and you will see that it leads everywhere and nowhere."

"How can that be?" he looks up at his grandfather, "Does this have something to do with the statue?"

"Yes. It has to do with the statue and much more." Phir Qi explains the phenomenon of the Parallel Planets and the importance of the inscriptions on the Sacred Oglala Crest. He finishes saying, "A Stableboy was sent here by mistake. Emera Softwind, my counterpart on Planet Theia caught him stealing the Sacred Oglala Crest, and cursed him here. He took a thoroughbred horse named 'Runs like the Wind', changed him into the statue and brought him here."

"Yeye? This is very complicated, you know, with the other planet and all that stuff. What does it have to do with me? Something was sent here from another planet, and, and I ... I have to get it back by February 29th or it's the end of the world. That's like a week away. Give me a break," he shakes his head, "I'm just a kid, and I don't want to save the world. You can do it; Dad can do it ... not me."

"Sūnzi, you are the Chosen One and with Xandr, your counterpart, you must ---" he stops and looks at Anza's quizzical expression.

"Chosen One? Counter what?" he looks at his grandfather, "and, who is Xandr, and why---?"

A voice coming from the path interrupts Anza, "It is your destiny. I will help. The answers are all right here if you ask."

Anza jumps back, "Who said that?"

A three dimensional face appears in the path and continues, "I am Knowledge. This is where you come for answers to questions that fulfill your destiny."

Anza looks up as he hugs his grandfather, "Yeye, I'm confused."

"Come Sūnzi, there's something I want to show you."

They walk to the house, through the kitchen, stopping only to grab a chocolate chip cookie, and continue to the Chamber Obscura.

Phir pauses, "Get the silver box," he instructs.

"I left it in the Chamber Obscura."

They enter the Grand Room and continue through the wall into the Chamber Obscura.

Anza stands by the podium with the silver box.

"There is a small compartment on the bottom, open it."

Anza turns the box over, and follows Phir's order.

"Turn the Rigui dial counterclockwise eight times to the number eight, and then clockwise three times back to the number eight. Lift the Peacock tail and slide it away from the dial."

"There are more rings like mine, except they have different kinds of stones."

"They belonged to your ancestors that were the Chosen One of their time. You will pass them on when it is time. Close the slide and turn the box back up. Look inside, there's something else in the box."

"Yeah, my Magical Transfer Ring."

"Remove your sun glasses and look again."

"Whoa! An iPad. I love it. I love it. How long's this been here?"

"Thousands of years."

"Thousands ... yeah right ... didn't they just invent ...? Now you're gonna tell me that it's magical."

Phir looks down at his grandson with a little smile; "Yes it is. It is *very* magical. It's an Oracle Frame; a seventh sense."

"A seventh sense? I've heard of sixth sense, but never seven. What does it do?"

"You will be able to talk to Xandr on Planet Theia."

"Are you gonna tell me who Xandr is?"

"He is the same as you, but does not have the powers you have as the Chosen One. The Oracle Frame will also help you read the Chronicle of Unchangeable Changes," Phir pauses a moment, "this is enough excitement for today. We will study more tomorrow. It's time for you to sleep."

"Don't we have to save the world today?"

"First, you have to learn *why* you are the Chosen One, what all of this means, and how you must deal with the challenge before you can take any action. Off to bed."

*   *   *   *   *   *   *

Qingling and Anza are finishing breakfast and begin to leave as Phir stops them saying, "Come back soon. You have lessons."

Anza, wearing his cool sunglasses and Qingling leave the house and run through the meadow. A slight breeze comes up in concert with harp-like music streaming through the tall grass. The kids stop and look around to see where the music is coming from. Frightened, they dart forward and come across the Path of Knowledge.

The Raven having morphed into an Owl is flying high above and watching.

Qingling stops with a swinging motion as Anza jumps aside. Qingling shouts out, "Whoa," looking down at the path changing to a green carpet, she spins around, "what's this place?" she looks at her cousin in disbelief, "where'd it ---?"

Surprised, Anza responds, "You can see it?"

"Yeahhhh," she stretches the word out, "where are we? Where did this path come from? It's never been here before."

"It's called the Path of Knowledge."

A voice coming from the Path interrupts Anza. "I am here to help you understand."

"Who said that?" Qingling says meekly.

"Here, look down," responds the Path.

A gentle smiling three-dimensional face rises from out of the Path, but is interrupted by two raccoons.

Two raccoons appear out of nowhere. The white one has a small sweet smile, while the black one looks a little sinister. The black raccoon speaks, "Hi, kids. I'm Notso."

Anza looks at Qingling. "Did that raccoon just ---?"

Qingling interrupts with, "I must be crazy; the ground talks, and that ... that raccoon ... naah."

The white raccoon does a little dance and says, "Hi, I'm Metoo."

"This is too much," says Qingling, "let's get outta here."

Qingling grabs Anza's hand as the kids turn and run away down the path toward Anza's house. They stop to catch their breath, and look around to see both raccoons right there beside them.

"Go to the old barn," Notso commands quietly.

The raccoons dematerialize, as the kids stand awestruck for a moment, and then continue running. The kids stop as they get to the house. Anza grabs Qingling's hand leading her inside. They go directly to Anza's room. Anza takes his Magical Transfer Ring out of its hiding place in the closet, and puts it on his finger.

Qingling watches, "Where'd you get that ---?"

Anza interrupts, "It's magical, come on," grabbing Qingling's hand.

They walk quickly to the Grand Room.

Qingling looks around, "I thought we were going to the old barn."

"Later, you gotta see this first."

Anza stops by the wall to the Chamber Obscura and starts waving his arms. He waits for the wall to open, but it does not.

Qingling looks bewildered, "What are ya doing?"

"It worked for Yeye. Open ... oh-h-h."

"What worked?"

"The Chamber Obscura; it's right here."

"Chamber what?"

"Quiet. Let me think."

Anza waves his arms again, stopping to point his Magical Transfer Ring, then waves more.

"Okay, okay. I got it now. Yeye spoke Chinese," he takes a deep breath and speaks 'open portal' in Chinese, "da-kai ménhu."

The wall becomes transparent as the Chamber Obscura appears.

"Whoa," shouts the big-eyed Qingling.

Anza grabs her hand and pulls her through the wall.

The surprised Qingling checks out the room stepping cautiously on the watery looking floor.

Anza points his ring finger at the Tome of Legends; it glows as the pages turn.

"What ... what is this?" Qingling asks.

"It's a magic tome."

"Tome?"

"It's a ... like a book."

The pages stop at a picture of a horse.

"That looks like the statue in the old barn ---"

Anza butts in, "I've got an idea. Let's go."

They run out of the room and go to the old barn.

*   *   *   *   *   *   *

Our line of vision beams in, as an enormous Stellar Monitor appears jutting out of the vaguely visible Portal Prompter showing scenes on Earth and Theia simultaneously. This phenomenon is more than your every day trans-travel.

On Planet Theia, Xandr Softwind and Yellowflower are standing in their Chamber Obscura. They watch as pages turn in the Chronicle of Unchangeable Changes. Xandr has his Magical Transfer Ring on the first finger of his left hand.

The diamond is shining a blue-green colored beam to the Chronicle of Unchangeable Changes as the pages stop.

We look back to Planet Earth on the Monitor.

*   *   *   *   *   *

Anza and Qingling cautiously enter the old barn and inspect the bronze horse.

The Raven is perched in the rafters watching.

Anza closes his eyes, points his ring finger and speaks 'come to life' twice in Chinese, "Lái shenghuó ... lái shenghuó."

The bronze statue sheds the metal coat slowly from its head down to its feet, comes alive and rears up as the kids jump back.

Surprised at what he just did, Anza proclaims, "It works, it works."

'Runs like the Wind' extends his foreleg and softly scratches the straw covered barn floor; he walks to Anza, nudges him and telepathically speaks to him, "Let's go for a ride."

"Yeah, okay ... cool," he responds aloud.

"Okay cool, what?"

"He wants to go for a ride."

"He wants you to ride him," Qingling turns around in circles, "the statue that almost looks real wants ---"

"Yes, he just told me."

"The horse spoke to you. I didn't hear anything."

"It was like ... like in my mind."

"So-o-o he didn't say anything, you just ... what? That's crazy. I gotta go. See ya."

Qingling turns and runs out of the barn. Anza grabs a three-legged stool, steps on it, mounts the horse and rides out as Qingling watches in amazement. The Raven flies out and follows Anza.

* * * * * * *

We return our sights to the Stellar Monitor. On Planet Theia, Xandr and Yellow Flower watch the glowing pages of the Chronicle of Unchangeable Changes turn and stop at a picture of the statue of 'Runs like the Wind' ... the image on the page changes, the horse becomes alive with Anza riding him away from the barn.

Yellowflower exclaims, "Whoa. What's happening?"

Xandr counters with, "That's my horse. How'd he get in there?"

"Where's there, and who's that riding him?"

They look at each other with blank stares.

* * * * * * *

In the Stellar Monitor, we look back to Earth...

Phir is waiting near the old barn with a grandfather's authoritarian hands-on-the-hips stance as Anza rides up on 'Runs like the Wind'.

"I did it, I made him real," Anza shouts as he reins in creating a dust vortex.

"Put him in the barn."

"But ---"

"No buts. Be sure he's a statue."

"How?"

"You knew how to make him real. Do the opposite and then come into the house."

"Am I in trouble?"

Phir turns away and goes into the house without another word as Anza slowly dismounts 'Runs like the Wind' and leads him into the barn.

"We'll go for a ride soon. I promise," he points his Magical Transfer Ring and cants 'return to a statue' in Chinese, "Fǎnhuí de diāoxiàng."

The bronze skin begins covering the horse starting at the hoofs and moving up to his head. He winks at Anza just before his eyes are covered, speaking telepathically, "Thanks for the ride."

Anza walks to the house with his head down as he hears his mother calling out, "Dinner."

"Hi mom, hi dad," looking at Phir he says quietly and dejectedly, "grandfather," he stretches it out.

"Wash your hands," Meilin Bancroft-Qi sings out in a motherly fashion as she looks at Phir, "Something going on with you and Anza?"

"Sūnzi is too fast with his lessons. He skips the important parts and doesn't like it when I try to get him back on track."

"What were you teaching him today?" asks Baxter Qi as he gets a weird 'none-of-your business' look from Phir, "What I mean is; a father has the right to know what studies his only son is pursuing."

Phir replies sarcastically, "Home schooling is not easy, especially the language of magic that you love."

"Bax was just ---"

A typical interruption, "I'm hungry as a horse," Anza sings out as he jumps around the country kitchen, stopping to quickly kiss his mom and dad on their cheeks and slide onto his chair.

"No kiss for Yeye?" his dad asks.

"I'm mad at him."

* * * * * * *

The next morning Anza decides to hook-up with cousins Arthur, Longwei and Qingling. He texts them to go to the countryside near the Path of Knowledge.

"It's right here ... it's here," Anza calls out.

Arthur responds as any twelve-year-old boy would, "What?"

"The Path; it's here," he points down to the dirt path.

Longwei, being a year older and smarter than Arthur, breaks in with, "Duh, we're here all the time. Can't you see it's right here, a dirt path?"

"No, listen to me. It's *THE* Path. Yeye showed me."

Arthur responds, "Come on let's go. He's getting all weird again."

"No, wait. It's called the Path of Knowledge. Q, help me, tell them."

Qingling shrugs her shoulders and looks at the others quizzically.

A slight breeze comes up in concert with harp-like music streaming through the tall grass, the path transforms, and then two raccoons materialize dancing on the path.

"Look at the path; it's like a carpet, and those raccoons. Where'd they come from?" Longwei shouts, "and ... they're dancing"

"Yup, we are dancing, 'cause we're happy to be on the Path of Knowledge," sings Metoo.

"Did that raccoon just talk?" asks Arthur.

Notso looks at Anza, "Magic is fun, huh?"

"You're trouble. Go away we've got things to do."

"I just want to help."

"Q and I have things to do; we'll catch up with you guys later." Anza says to the boys.

Qingling looks at Anza and quietly says, "I gotta get home, I'll see you later."

* * * * * * *

Duo activates a dual screen on the Stellar Portal Prompter. We see Phir and Anza in the Chamber Obscura studying at the podium while Emera and Xandr are doing the same on the Planet Theia.

Phir and Emera are passing the *Conscientiousness of the Ages* to their grandsons in a synchronistical fashion; the Tome of Legends is on Planet Earth and the Chronicle of Unchangeable Changes is on Planet Theia.

Phir speaks softly, but with determination, "This book, the Tome of Legends, belongs on the other planet that I told you about. Do you remember?"

"Yes, it's called Theia and is on the other side of the Sun so we can't see it."

"Yes my little Sūnzi. The people that live there, our counterparts, are like us, but they look a little different, and have a book called the Chronicle of Unchangeable Changes, which belongs here on Earth."

"Why are the books in the wrong places?"

"Things got mixed up. Theia has developed one hundred years slower than Earth and Nous switched the books' locations on purpose so they would not fall into the wrong hands. The Tome of Legends can only be interpreted by our counterparts on Planet Theia, and the Chronicle of Unchangeable Changes can only be read by second generation males in our family."

"You and me ... not dad."

"Until you and Xandr learn, it's just me and Xandr's grandfather Emera."

"Who is Nous, and how can we read the Tome of Legends if it's on the other planet?"

Phir Qi purposely avoids the question about Nous answering, "The Sacred Oglala Crest has a stone in its center that was touched by a Sacred Calf Pipe and given special powers by a Lakota Medicine Man who was Nous' Apprentice. There are inscriptions on the Crest that can only be deciphered using a Magical Transfer Ring. When it is decoded it will become a Magnifying Cipher Glass, which is the secret key to read the Tome of Legends."

"What about the Chronicle of Unchangeable Changes? How is it read?"

"The Crest's counterpart is the Cosmic Eye Medallion and is the key to read the Chronicle of Unchangeable Changes."

"Medallion? Where is it and when do I learn to use it?"

"Trust me Sūnzi. You will learn soon enough."

* * * * * * *

We return our sights to the Stellar Monitor. On Planet Theia, we hear Emera, "Trust me Tȟakóža."

* * * * * * *

We look back to Earth and understand that human intelligence was not transferred from Dimitri Talbot to the Raven during the curse, which requires the Raven to call upon Dimitri for advice.

The Raven is sitting on a rock by the pool in the cave where he has hidden the Crest, "Where are you," he calls out to the pool?

An image of Dimitri appears in the pond and speaks, "Have you found the Tome of Legends?"

"It's somewhere in the house. I saw the boy carrying a silver box go through an invisible opening in the wall with his grandfather."

"Invisible opening? What do you mean?"

"The grandfather waved his hands and shouted some strange words. They sort of disappeared after they went through the wall and ---"

Dimitri's image in the pool interrupts, "Chinese."

"Chinese?" the Raven squawks, "Chinese ... Chinese."

"Did you see anything?"

"No, nothing."

"You've got to find a way through the wall. The Tome of Legends must be there."

* * * * * * *

Anza and his cousins are walking and jumping as they move along the Path of Knowledge. The Raccoons appear mimicking them.

Anza shouts, "What are you raccoons doing here?"

Metoo responds, "Hi. I'm Metoo, he's Notso."

"Oh-hh, I think that I'm going crazy."

"We're here to help you save the world."

"You can help? What do you know about saving the world?"

"We cannot save the world but, we have seen many things," Metoo points up, "watch there, in the sky."

Chapter Two

The Equilibrium

A transparent Stellar Bubble Craft appears as a dot in the sky becoming larger and larger as it moves faster than rocket speed toward Earth causing a tremendous vibration.

The Craft stops instantly and silently about two feet above the ground just a few feet from the kids.

A golden glow surrounds the Craft as a doorway appears in the outer shell illuminating the interior in silvery light. A childlike soft pale-green ethereal Being floats through the doorway of the glass-like surface. The Being, clothed in a lavender silk pirate-like shirt, baggy cinched purple ankle trousers and white sandals, surrounded by the silvery light, remains suspended above the ground as the craft speeds away into space.

The kids gasp in bewilderment.

The smiling ethereal Being sits Buddha style two feet above the ground, with legs crossed and speaks in a child-like voice, "I am called Nous. I come from the interstitial world of Anon."

Anza stares at this child-like wonder, "Inter what?"

"It's a four-dimensional world."

Longwei pipes in, "4D, I thought there's only 3D."

"The four-dimensional world is a composite of your two worlds."

Arthur looks puzzled and turns to Anza, "Two worlds? Do you know about this?"

"Sort of."

Metoo jumps up and down, "Tell them, tell them."

Nous looks at the raccoon and then the kids, "I am the keeper of planetary balance. I am the Equilibrium."

The kids look quizzically at each other.

"Your planet has received a person and some objects that belong on your parallel planet."

Andrew begins to interrupt, but Nous makes an ethereal gesture, which magically silences him.

Nous continues, "There is another planet called Theia, which is on the other side of the Sun where you cannot see it. It is like your Earth; Anza can tell you more about Theia another time."

Nous studies the kids' faces, "For now all you need to know is that a horse with a white saddle and a special crest was turned into a statue, and a stable boy was turned into a raven. They were sent to Earth from Theia, which caused the planets to be out of balance."

The kids look at Nous and each other in bewilderment.

"These objects must be returned before the next February twenty-ninth or there will be chaos." Nous hesitates and slowly scans the faces of the puzzled kids, "Anza will need your help to return these items back to their rightful place in the universe. Think about what I have said. I will return to the Path of Knowledge when the Chosen One," looking at Anza, "summons me."

With a gesture, the Stellar Bubble Craft appears in the sky, swoops in, and stops short of the kids hovering near Nous. The outer shell doorway opens discharging its silvery light that joins with the light that is encompassing the Being drawing it back inside and rockets away in a silent hyperdrive as it disappears into space.

"That was cool," exclaims Qingling.

"Cool," resounds Longwei turning to Anza, "Okay, oh chosen one, so what's next? February twenty-ninth is not that far away."

Arthur, with a serious look asks Anza, "Why do we have to do anything if that guy is the keeper of all this planet balance stuff?"

"Dunno. I gotta talk to Yeye."

* * * * * * *

The Raven returns to the cave where he has hidden the Crest and is shouting at the pool, "Where are you? We must talk."

Dimitri's image appears in the pool, "You felt it?"

"Yes. The Equilibrium has appeared to the children."

"We must mobilize our resources and get the Tome."

"Resources?"

"Go to Carl Drinkwater."

"Who's that?"

"He's the same as me ... us; he's our counterpart here. He can help."

"Is that all?"

"Go to the old barn; you'll be able to transform into your human image. Speak the words 'Yuto Keca Vicasa' twice. The transformation only works for a few moments at a time so talk quickly and explain to Drinkwater what we need him to do."

"And-d-d ... what exactly is that ... my disembodied alter ego?"

Chapter Three

The Space-Between Dimensions

Totfote materializes and we climb aboard for our trip to the Space-Between Dimensions. Solo leads the way; we sit in an open cabin directly behind the pilot and navigator. XR activates, and we are ready.

Solo instructs, "Let's go."

Duo commands with authority, "Data 5168," and his Universal Portal Prompter materializes. His fingers respond to the information as they flash back and forth across the futuristic keypad. Totfote transforms into a transparent cylinder spacecraft. Duo strikes a freshly illuminated icon as the Portal Prompter displays a glowing three-dimensional image, "Fold space-time."

Solo strikes another pad at the command center, and suddenly with a soul-wrenching blast, the Portal Prompter expands sucking us into it; *we* find ourselves traveling through a space-time continuum arriving on the outskirts of the four-dimensional world of Anon. Our ship hovers high above. It is pitch black, but we can see a portion of the four-dimensional world.

A bolt of lightning shatters the blackness illuminating the four-dimensional world for a split second.

"What was that?" shouts one of our interlopers.

"Silence; Daiyu is displaying anger."

"Who?" asks another Interloper.

Solo explains, "Daiyu, also known as the Black Jade, is an outcast from the four-dimensional planet of Anon and lives in the Space-Between Dimensions. We have encountered his wrath during previous travels."

An entity shaped like a ghostly human form is flying like a human space ship back and forth between Earth and Theia at the speed of a super-charged rocket. The form stops for a brief moment at each planet, then moves back to the Space-Between Dimensions. This unusual vessel seems to have mastered trans-dimensional travel.

Our line of vision beams in on an enormous Stellar Monitor jutting out of the Portal Prompter that shows Nous on Earth and then on Theia simultaneously.

The Black Jade turns and fires a lightening bolt in our direction; it seems to travel straight toward us, but somehow, in the last moment, it is on a diverted path past our Starcruiser continuing its flight into the never-ending space beyond.

"Time to go," orders Solo, "we may not be able to redirect any more hyper-trans attacks with our Stealth Averteron," Solo looks at Duo and commands, "Activate Stealth Slot Mode."

Without a reply, Duo keyboards the Portal Prompter. Our Starcruiser blasts forward like it did before as Solo engages the command center.

We fold through space-time and slide into an energy-field surrounded Stealth Slot in an instant.

"We will be safe here," Duo assures us.

It seems that we are in a synchronistic environment. We view Earth and Theia at the same time. The Stellar Monitor warps into a semi-circular one hundred eighty-degree transparent glass-like futuristic monitor.

Solo looks at us and says, "You may move about as we watch what is happening. Duo will direct the focal point to our particular subjects on Earth and Theia." The XR disengages and we move about.

Looking in one direction, we see Anza, his father Baxter, his mother Meilin, and Phir at the dinner table. In the opposite direction, we see Xandr, his father Lone Eagle, his mother Moonshadow, and grandfather Emera at *their* dinner table. All that is happening on Earth is happening on Theia and vice versa.

Solo instructs Duo, "Activate Earth trans-audio, and silence Theia duplicate audio transmission."

Meilin looks up from her dinner and asks Anza, "What have you been doing today?"

Anza looks to his grandfather for assistance, but Phir looks away, "Yeye has been helping me with my lessons, and ... and I played with cousins on the Path."

Baxter looks up, "What path?"

"You know, down in the meadow."

"In the meadow? Have you two been up to something?"

Phir keeps his head down, "Just teaching the boy about nature. We're going to have more lessons after he's done with the dishes."

Baxter shakes his fork like a conductor directing an orchestra and says, "Please don't teach him how to fly or any of your other ---"

Anza interrupts, "You can fly, Yeye?"

"Your father is joking," he responds looking at Baxter Qi with an evil eye.

We look the other way on the Stellar Monitor to planet Theia as Duo engages the trans-audio and we hear Xandr, "You can fly?"

Solo looks back at us, the Interlopers, and says, "Let's watch and see if he can fly."

Xandr and his Grandfather Emera Softwind leave the kitchen and walk down the road stopping at the edge of the Forest of Understanding as it materializes; the Forest of Understanding is the counterpart to the Path of Knowledge on Earth.

Emera, carrying his ceremonial Vision Quest Cane with a Tribal Waluta at the top, looks at Xandr and says, "Because there has been a great un-happening in the universe we must be ready to act with our counterparts on the Planet Earth."

Xandr starts to speak, but stops as Emera raises the Vision Quest Cane. The Tribal Waluta on top begins to unfurl even though there is no breeze at all. He grabs Emera's arm, as they are whisked-up in a mini tornado-like funnel. They fly to the stable, transform to a liquid form, and pass through the roof; returning to their original selves landing in the center of a large space.

Xandr looks at Emera in wonderment, "What ---?"

Emera gently pushes Xandr's chin up, "Magic my little Thakóža. It's magic. Come, I want to tell you a story."

Emera raises his cane again and a hoop appears on the stable floor, "Sit inside the cangleška wakan," he points, "the sacred hoop is a symbol of solidarity. Here we have a link between time and space."

"This is gonna be about the ---"

Emera puts his finger to Xandr's lips, "A long time ago somewhere in the beginning of our solar system two planets collided forming parallel worlds of Theia and Earth with almost identical occupants ---"

Time, as we know it, passes and Emera finishes, "We are in an unbalanced situation, which must be corrected by Anza with your help, or it will destroy both worlds."

"Does Anza look like me?"

"No. He is the same age, but of another ancestry."

Emera raises his cane. A holographic image of Anza sitting inside a circle of stones in the old Qi barn appears. Emera lowers his Cane before Xandr can say anything, and Anza's likeness dissolves into images of Dimitri and 'Runs like the Wind'.

"Look here Thakóža," he points, "see the stable boy, Dimitri? He stole the Sacred Oglala Crest and I sent him to Earth as a raven. He changed 'Runs like the Wind' into a statue and took him along to the other world with the Sacred Oglala Crest."

"That was the explosion we heard. That's when my horse disappeared."

"In my anger I created an imbalance that must be reversed. Any imbalance left unattended will create chaos and destruction in both worlds."

"Why can't you just change it back?"

"I have no powers on Planet Earth. Only the Chosen One can make the change and send them back."

Emera raises his cane, the Tribal Waluta flutters softly and the holographic image of Anza reappears.

"Is that Anza? Can we talk?"

"Yes, that is Anza. I'll show you how you can speak with him another time. You have much to learn first."

"What happens when Ate and Huku find out?"

"Your Dad and Mom will find out soon enough. Let's not rush it."

"Can I get my horse back?"

"He *must* come back."

* * * * * * *

Solo looks back at us, the interlopers, and says, "Now we know he can fly," he looks at his navigator, "activate Earth trans-audio-video, and exit the Theia duplicate audio-video transmission."

Duo points to a diagram on the screen touching a series of icons. We hear voices from Earth and see Anza and his grandfather walking along the Path of Knowledge.

It is a chilly day and Phir is wearing a classic Chinese dragon shawl that seems to be hiding something.

"Yeye? Who is Nous?"

"Nous? Ah, yes. You asked before and ... well, now is as good a time as any," he pauses, "you saw?"

"He, it... appeared to us right here on the path."

"The Equilibrium Child will only appear when the planets are imbalanced."

"He .. it... ? What is Nous, a boy or girl?"

"Nous is an Epicene lacking any gender distinction and is said to descend from the Ordering Force that formed the world out of the original chaos, and is the keeper of balance."

"Wow, and he said I can call him when ---"

Phir pulls a large colorful bow from under his dragon shawl.

"Where did you get that bow?"

"From the Chamber Obscura; it was sent from Theia with the Tome of Legends."

"If it's from the other planet then ---"

"Its counterpart, a Vision Quest Cane, was sent there and altered to be used magically. This is a Sacred Oglala Bow. It was handed down by Xandr's ancestor Black Road, a real medicine man and magician."

"What is that furry thing on top?"

"It's from a long tailed deer. It adds powerful magic from the Thunder Beings."

"Who are the Thunder Beings? What kind of magic?"

Phir Qi lifts the bow high up. The deer's tail waves and there is a great vibration with a thunderous clap. Phir, with his arm around Anza, rises up and they fly from the Path of Knowledge over the rooftops, transform into a fluid form and fly through the roof into the old barn; becoming their original selves as they land.

Phir and Anza are sitting on the straw covered floor inside a circle of stones as Phir finishes his story, "Or it will destroy both worlds."

"You mean like totally gone?"

"It is time for you to meet Xandr." Phir lifts the Sacred Bow again, but this time he slowly lowers it pointing to the center of the circle of stones. A hologram materializes with images of Xandr and Emera.

"Is that Xandr?"

"Yes and his grandfather Emera." Phir speaks to the hologram, "Emera. Can you hear me?"

The image responds, "Yes Phir, we do."

Phir introduces the boys explaining their relationship and the task they must accomplish.

Chapter Four

The Immortal Unknown

Solo readies the Starcruiser to depart our synchronistic environment for another voyage.

One of the Interlopers looks over Solo's shoulder and asks, "Where are we going now?"

Solo gets up from the pilot's seat and leads us away from the command center to our seats in the open cabin directly behind the pilot and navigator.

Solo instructs, "Secure passengers." Duo responds with a touch to the keypad and XR engages. "We will depart for an extraordinary trip to the Residence of the Most High." Solo looks at Duo and utters a quiet command, "Let's go."

Duo commands with authority, "Data 0001," and his Universal Portal Prompter materializes. His fingers fly across the futuristic keypad, as Totfote once again transforms into a transparent cylinder spacecraft. Duo strikes an illuminated icon as the Prompter shows a glowing four-dimensional image of the Residence of the Most High on Anon, "Fold space-time."

Solo strikes another control at the command center. Suddenly the Portal Prompter begins glowing with an exhilarating and soul warming feeling. A spinning deep-purple-colored Synchro Gateway appears; expanding larger, and larger, until it lifts us gently inside the Ethereal Cortex where we find ourselves traveling through a totally different type of space-time continuum, with sounds and vibrations that only an angelic chorus could have created within the ever-changing rainbows that encircle us on all sides.

The vibrations cease and the rainbows dissipate as we arrive at the massive entrance to the Residence of the Most High on the four-dimensional world of Anon. The Residence of the Most High is a never-ending combination of architectural styles we have seen on Earth and Theia along with styles we have never seen. The entrance has nine gigantic platinum and crystal multi-striated columns that begin as a pinpoint at an imaginary foundation widening to a mushroom-like top where they join a thousand or more feet above.

Our Starcruiser hovers and slowly lowers to the level of an imaginary landing platform. XR disengages as Totfote evaporates and we instinctively stand up. Without thinking, we walk between the columns to the massive light blue diamond-like faceted wall, which seems to be alive. Suddenly the wall opens with a deep sigh as massive crystal doors swing away and we are invited in by a translucent seven-foot tall humanoid Grey Form that cautions us, by telepathic communication, to be silent as we eagerly pass through the entrance.

As we move, it becomes apparent we are in a space like no other. The floor seems to be non-existent even though we are on a solid footing. The walls appear different from the outside; built of transparent crystal-like triangular stones set in a variable algorithmic string pattern that seems to be breathing in and out causing the high ceiling to raise and lower with celestial music surrounding us as we move. The music slows as we slow down and speeds up as we move faster. The ceiling changes hues as rainbow-like colors change with our every move.

We cover a vast distance in what seems to be a short time having a crystal-clear realization that something wonderful will soon happen; and it does.

An eight-foot tall surreal translucent light-blue humanoid form materializes gazing into a see-all Cosmos Comprehender, a celestial three-dimensional screen of the galaxy. We instinctively know it is Anon, the Immortal Unknown.

We quietly watch as the Comprehender displays a variety of actions including the transference of Dimitri Talbot and the Bronze Statue with shock waves radiating around Earth and Theia. A simultaneous zoom-in of Anza-Phir and Xandr-Emera becomes center screen. Two Grey Forms take their place at Anon's left side.

Anon speaks in a soft and distinctively authoritarian voice, "There has not been such an imbalance in millenniums," glancing back at us without any sort of acknowledgement, He continues, "there is something in addition to the transference of the boy and statue causing this chaos."

Grey Form One bows to Anon, "Great Immortal Unknown; the Sacred Oglala Crest was sent to Planet Earth with the horse."

Anon motions for Grey Form One to rise up, "Does anyone on the Earth Planet beside Phir Qi know how to use the Sacred Crest?"

"Phir Qi is in the process of passing his legacy on to his grandson, Anza."

"Will Anza be ready?"

"He will be; with the help of Phir Qi."

"Anyone else qualified?"

"No. The Stableboy," Grey Form One pauses, "now a raven, has hidden the Crest, and is plotting to steal the Tome of Legends."

"Is the Sacred Oglala Crest's Counterpart safe?"

Grey Form Two bows to Anon, "Great Immortal Unknown; the Cosmic Eye Medallion is safe in a secret compartment within the Tome of Legends' podium."

Anon motions for Grey Form Two to rise up, "The Medallion would certainly be in jeopardy if the Raven is successful in his quest for the Tome."

Grey Form One responds, "There would surely be chaos for Earth and Theia."

"They can only judge by the experiences of ordinary life. How insecure they are to interfere with natural principles using only the light of common knowledge and subjective ideas."

The Grey Forms bow in acknowledgement.

Anon gestures to the Grey Forms, "Summon Nous and," Anon pauses pointing to us, "RSR them if they wish to continue."

The Grey Forms bow and turn away from Anon.

Grey Form Two looks down at us, "You and your spacecraft must undergo the RSR if you wish to continue your venture here or you will certainly face destruction."

Our mental message responds in unison, "We want to continue. What is RSR?"

"It is the Replication Synchronization Ritual. All Interlopers must go through a process of producing an identical copy from one original DNA molecule in order for you to visit both planets simultaneously. Your spacecraft will go through a similar process. You must be synchronized or you will add to the chaos. We will escort you to the Replication Synchronization Nebula."

Without further ado, the awesome Grey Forms lead us out through the massive entrance, back through the Portal Prompter and down a crystallized path lined with closely anchored alternating blue and white internally lit translucent ten feet tall bamboo shoots. A mysterious force captures us, and instantly transports us the length of the path to a distant knoll.

Sitting atop the knoll is the Pearl Pavilion, the ultimate Replication Synchronization Nebula, a massive silver-white cloud-like building, which is rising from beneath the ground directly in front of us as if it knew we were coming. An Intelligent multi-colored Portal bursts out from the outer shell forming a unique fractured opening inviting us to enter. Once we are inside the opening closes with a whooshing sound.

We find ourselves inside the Intermix Chamber, which appears as a never-ending space. Pentagonal strands bounce around bonding with each other forming strands that go in all directions and finally into a dual forking where they replicate themselves.

Watch out! Too late, swallowed up by a Helicase, which unwinds the strands, we get twisted and turned as the strands around us separate forming bubbles that are receiving our DNA proteins in segments resulting in human forms that mirror our existence.

Our replicated forms move away into the duplicate of our spacecraft, Etoftot, and speed away from the Intermix Chamber at hyperdrive. The Helicase dissolves and we are lead out of the Intermix Chamber.

A mysterious force captures us and positions us in our spacecraft. Aboard Totfote and without any action from

Solo or Duo we instantly find ourselves landing on Earth. Our Starcruiser dematerializes near the old barn.

We have a cosmic feeling we are moving in opposite directions at one time, and are somewhere in addition to Earth. Solo tells us that our replicas will be transported simultaneously aboard the duplicate Starcruiser Etoftot to Planet Theia.

Everything seems to be the same for our replicas, except ... the duplicate Starcruiser is a mirror image of itself. After close inspection, we realize that we too, as duplicates, are like a parallel, but opposite image.

We wonder what the Replication Synchronization Ritual has done and if we will ever be the same.

Chapter Five

The Chamber Obscura

The Raven watches in the shadowy evening light outside the old Qi barn as his earthly counterpart, the weather beaten Carl Drinkwater enters. The Raven looks around to see if anyone else is around. Satisfied, he flies into the barn and sees Carl examining the bronze statue. He calls out, "Carl. Carl Drinkwater."

Carl looks around, sees nothing, shakes his head and continues his inspection.

"Carl, look over here."

"Who's there?" He sees the Raven, "get outta here bird." He picks up a riding crop and swings it at the Raven who flies away and settles down on a hay bale.

The Raven speaks the words 'change to man' twice in a Lakota tongue, "Yuto keca vicasa, yuto keca vicasa," and morphs into an image of Dimitri Talbot, "Don't be afraid. My name is Dimitri Talbot, and I am from the parallel world Theia."

"Parallel world? You got somtin' to do with this here statue?"

"I need your help to get the book from the secret room in the house."

"I am not allowed in the big house."

"But you must ---"

Carl interrupts, "You should talk to Mister Nigel."

Dimitri changes back to the Raven and flies off to spy on Anza with hope to find the Tome of Legends. He perches on the sill of the Grand Room window and waits until he sees Anza and Phir go through the wall into the Chamber Obscura.

Anza and Phir are standing at the glass podium in the Chamber Obscura. Anza looks over his shoulder and sees his mother and father enter the great room.

"Look, Yeye it's mom and dad."

"Don't worry, they can't see us."

"Don't they know about this place?"

"No. Just you and me."

"The Raven is looking in the window."

"He doesn't know about this place. Does he?" asks Phir

Anza gets fidgety.

"What's wrong? Have you been here without me?"

"Just with Q."

"Did the Raven see you come here?"

"I don't know."

"You should not be here without me until you are ready; there is great power here. Be careful, you will have powers you won't understand."

"Like you have with the Bow? I can go to the Path if I don't understand," he looks down, "right?"

"How did you get in here? Never mind. You learn fast, but understanding is one thing; *control* is everything. You must learn how to control your new powers."

"When you teach me about the Bow and the Seventh Sense, I mean Oracle Frame; will I be able to fly to the other world?"

Phir Qi ignores the question, "Your lessons continue now. First, you must remember that you cannot read the Tome of Legends. It is an instrument of transference to read the Chronicle of Unchangeable Changes, which is in the other world."

"Why not ...?" Anza begins.

Phir interrupts, "I am the only one on Earth that has the gift to use the Tome of Legends to read the Chronicle of Unchangeable Changes for now."

"You taught me the I Ching, the Book of Changes. How can the other one be Unchangeable Changes?"

"In order to understand you must Paesre."

"Paesre? Where is that?"

"It's not a place, it's here, inside." Phir touches the center of Anza's chest and forehead simultaneously. "It's all about space without the restrictions of time. It is another dimension. It's trans-dimensional where you become one with the Universe; one with the Center of Consciousness, and move about without affecting time as you know it." He smiles with an enlightened smile, knowing Anza will soon be ready to take his place as the Chosen One, "It is a place where there is no past, no present, no future."

"No future? Move about? Like flying?"

"You must hear and understand what I say. It is more than moving about and flying. It is living in conscious harmony with nature's way, to transfer your entire being to another place and remain here simultaneously. First, you must understand the great responsibility that comes with your legacy. It is time for your lessons. February 29th will be here soon. We must hurry."

* * * * * * *

Carl Drinkwater is sitting on a bale of hay in the old Qi barn as the brawny foreman, Nigel Churchill, walks through the open doorway wearing blue jeans, matching jacket, boots and a cowboy hat.

"Hello Carl."

The surprised Carl jumps up, "Mister Nigel. I, uh."

"You have been spending a lot of time in this old barn." Nigel spots the statue, "What is this?"

"It's nothing sir, jest sometin I found."

"Just where did you find it? Never mind. What is it doing here?"

The Raven flies in and perches in the rafters. Nigel looks up and sees the Raven, "Never seen a raven in these parts."

"He's from somewhere else."

"And just where would that be?"

"Same place as the statue."

The Raven flies down, morphs into Dimitri and stands next to the statue. Nigel jumps back, grabs a pitchfork and stands ready for battle.

Dimitri points to himself and the statue, "We're from the other world."

Nigel cautiously looks around, "How'd you do that? What other world? "

"It's magic," he lies, and changes the subject. "The parallel world is on the other side of the sun."

"I've heard stories of another world, but thought they were just folklore."

"I need your help to get the Tome of Legends from a secret room in the big house."

"Tome of ...? Secret room? I do not want to be a part of your plan to steal from the Qi's," Nigel lies, "go, leave me."

Dimitri morphs back into the Raven and flies out of the barn.

Nigel Churchill, realizing there is more to this than meets the eye, dials his mobile phone, "Gather the hands and meet me at the corral."

Chapter Six

The Negative Presence

Solo, studying the Stellar Monitor, looks up at Duo and says, "Something is happening on Planet Theia." Solo readies the position of our Starcruiser to depart our synchronistic environment for a new voyage experience.

One of the Interlopers looks over Solo's shoulder and asks, "Where are we going now?"

Solo gets up from the pilot's seat and leads us away from the command center, "Sit in your assigned seats."

Solo instructs, "Secure passengers." Duo responds with a touch to the keypad and XR engages. Our replicated forms and the duplicate of our spacecraft, Etoftot, are sitting in readiness. "We will depart for an extraordinary trip to Theia." Solo looks at Duo and utters a quiet command, "Transfer into RSR mode."

Duo commands with authority, "Data 84342," and his Universal Portal Prompter materializes. His fingers fly across the futuristic keypad and he sounds out, "Data RSR777," as Totfote and its passengers slowly dematerialize. Duo strikes the remaining icon on the Prompter. "Fold synchronistic trans-conversion."

We find ourselves, aboard our duplicate Starcruiser Etoftot instantly materializing on Planet Theia. XR disengages; we instinctively stand up as our synchronistic Starcruiser evaporates leaving us in this extraordinary situation as a reverse duplicate of ourselves.

We look around and see Nicholas Gray Wolf in the distance; a man we will soon find to be the counterpart of Nigel Churchill, another archenemy of Anza. Anza must defeat him in his quest to return the Sacred Oglala Crest, the horse and the raven to Planet Theia.

The ruddy-complected Nicholas Gray Wolf, Softwind farm foreman, is riding his horse on a dirt road as four Lakota Indian bad guys on horseback come up alongside. Gray Wolf motions and they follow for a short ride. They dismount in front of an abandoned Way Station. Gray Wolf goes inside with the bad guys following close behind.

The one room cabin is clean; furnished with a table and four chairs, a cot, a fireplace with pots hanging from the mantel and a sink with cupboards above. The bad guys look around in amazement.

Gray Wolf sizes them up, "There's whiskey and glasses in the cupboard."

The small bad guy speaks first, "Not what it looks like from outside. You fix it up like dis?"

Gray Wolf smiles as the big 'in-charge' bad guy grabs a bottle and some glasses and sets them on the table with a thud. He opens the bottle and pours a drink, slams the bottle of 'Firewater' on the table, pulls out a chair and sits down. He raises his glass to Gray Wolf, "What's going on? What do you want us for?"

Gray Wolf sits on the table's edge, "The stable boy stole a crest from the Softwind Farm. It is said to have great magic and hold the key to treasures beyond belief."

The small bad guy says, "Where's he at? Do you want us to rough him up and take it?"

"Yeah ... yeah," sounds come from the other bad guys.

"It ain't gonna be that easy."

The bad guys look at Gray Wolf. They down a couple of drinks and wait for him to speak.

Gray Wolf breaks the silence knowing his cohorts would not understand, "I saw Emera Softwind put a curse on the Stableboy and send him to the other world."

The bad guys look at each other.

The small bad guy speculates, "Udder world? He kill 'em and sent 'em down der?" he points down.

With a smug look, Gray Wolf responds, "You've heard of Earth, the other world, haven't you?"

The bad guys shake their heads yes, but shrug their shoulders in disbelief looking at each other.

Finally, the small bad guy says, "Yeah. But, them's jest stories. There ain't no setch place. There ain't, ere they?"

Gray Wolf assures them, "Yes, there is, and we'll be going there to get the treasure."

"We'll be going there?" the 'in-charge' bad guy asks, "How do we get to this here other world place?"

"Black Elk is bringing a medicine man that will send us there."

An hour later Gray Wolf and the Bad Guys, quite liquored-up, are still sitting at the table as Black Elk comes into the cabin carrying a colorful bow and pulling an old Indian man whose hands are tied up.

He pushes him to the corner, "Sit there," as he stands the bow against the wall next to the door jamb.

"Who's the Injun?" asks the 'in-charge' bad guy.

"He's Running Bear, the medicine man. He has the power to get us to the other world."

"How old's he? Dun't look like he can do no medsin man magic," snickers the small bad guy.

Black Elk assures the men, "I told him I'd hurt his granddaughter if he didn't get us there. Untie him and bring him here to me."

The 'in-charge' bad guy motions. Two bad guys get up, grab the old Indian, untie him, pull him to the table and push him down on a chair.

Gray Wolf looks unemotionally at Running Bear, "We are ready to go to the other world."

Running Bear shakes his head no.

"Remember what I said?"

Running Bear pleads, "Hiya oyazove mitakoja ki."

"What's he sayin'?" asks the small bad guy.

"He said not to hurt his grandchild." Nicholas Gray Wolf responds as he looks at Running Bear, "Hiya oyazove ... you do wikasa ... magic."

Running Bear stares puzzled as Gray Wolf draws imaginary circles around himself and the bad guys; then he points away to the sky.

"Makoce ... ha ... ha makoce," calls out Running Bear.

The small bad guy stands, "He's laughin' at us. I'll ---"

"Ha means yes, makoce is earth," assures Gray Wolf.

Running Bear points to the colorful bow propped up against the wall. Gray Wolf grabs the bow and hands it to him. Running Bear stands and raises the bow toward the ceiling. He begins performing a ceremonial Indian dance as he sings out unintelligible Lakota words while raising the bow. Suddenly, a mini twister forms around Gray Wolf and the Bad Guys. The twister increases in speed with a deafening sound like a train was coming into the cabin.

The Way Station door blows off its hinges as a sonic boom shatters the room. Gray Wolf and the bad guys are caught up in the twister and swept out the open doorway and into outer space.

* * * * * * *

Solo instructs, "Secure yourselves."

The duplicate of our Starcruiser materializes and we, as our replicated forms, hop aboard and sit in readiness.

"We will depart for our return to Earth." Solo looks at Duo and utters a quiet command, "Transfer into RSR mode. Secure passengers."

XR engages as Duo commands with authority, "Data 32784," and his Universal Portal Prompter materializes. His fingers fly across the futuristic keypad, and he sounds out, "data RSR777," as we slowly dematerialize along with our Starcruiser. Duo strikes the remaining icon on the Portal Prompter, "Fold synchronistic trans-conversion."

We find ourselves, and our Starcruiser instantly materializing on Planet Earth as our original selves. XR disengages and we instinctively stand up as our Starcruiser dematerializes.

There is a thunderous sound as Gray Wolf and the bad guys materialize a short distance from the Qi farmhouse with amazement.

"What the ...?" hollers the small bad guy.

Gray Wolf speaks with authority, "We have arrived at the other world. Let's look around."

"What er we looking fer?" asks the small bad guy.

"I saw the stable boy change the stallion into a bronze statue ... the magical crest should be with the saddle."

"The stable," he exclaims as he points, "over there ... that's where the horse should be."

"That's too obvious. Let's look there in the old barn."

* * * * * * *

Nigel Churchill and his farm hands are riding from the corral to their normal gathering place at the foot of the hills when they witness the arrival of Gray Wolf and his band of outlaw Indians.

Anza, Qingling, Arthur, and Longwei are on the Path of Knowledge when the transference thunderbolt strikes and the ground shakes indicating the arrival of the others from Planet Theia. The sky grows dim for a moment and the wind stops. The trees are still and the birds stop singing. All is quiet and peaceful.

The kids hear the sound and feel the shock wave.

Longwei looks at the others, "That sounds like trouble."

Anza puts his finger to his lips, "Shh ... listen."

"I don't hear anything," whispers Qingling.

"That's the problem. It's happening again."

Longwei asks, "What's happening?"

"Another," Qingling questions, "something from the other Planet?"

It's Arthur's turn, "Or maybe someone."

"We gotta find Yeye," shouts the apprehensive Anza.

* * * * * * *

Gray Wolf and the bad guys search the Qi's old barn while the Raven watches from the rafters.

The small bad guy yells with excitement, "Over here."

Gray Wolf and the other bad guys rush to the statue.

"That's it. That's 'Runs like the Wind', Gray Wolf shouts, as he pushes the others out of the way, "Let's get the Crest from the saddle and get outta here."

Gray Wolf finds the vacant spot on the saddle, "This is where it should be."

The bad guys look skeptically at each other.

The 'in-charge' bad guy asks, "Where do we look now? We come here to dis other world to find our fortune and...," frustrated he looks with an evil eye to Gray Wolf as he puffs up his chest. "You got any other bright ideas?"

"We gotta ---" Gray Wolf starts to speak, but is interrupted by a voice from the rafters.

The Raven swoops down landing on a hay bale, "No need to look. I have the Crest."

The bad guys look around to see who is talking.

"I'm here," says the Raven.

They look at the Raven.

The small bad guy asks, "'Dat bird just talk?"

The Raven morphs into Dimitri surprising Gray Wolf and the bad guys. They jump back and look at Dimitri in astonishment. Gray Wolf pulls his revolver from its holster and points it at Dimitri.

"No need for the gun. You're here for the Crest, but it's too late," he lies, "I've made a deal with someone else."

"I'll double whatever you've been promised. What do you want?" Gray Wolf waves his gun.

"I want my own ranch with hundreds of horses, a beautiful loving wife and more money than I can spend." He sizes up Gray Wolf with an unsettling scowl, "Can you do better than that?" Dimitri doesn't wait for an answer and changes back to the Raven and flies away.

Gray Wolf holsters his gun shouting, "Wait, wait."

* * * * * * *

Solo and Duo go through their procedure and we find ourselves seated in our Starcruiser on a trip to a place we visited before, but never stayed long enough to investigate. Traveling trans-dimensionally, we arrive almost immediately at the outer reaches of the four-dimensional world of Anon, to a space that is not in or out of any world, but is a portal to the outcast Space-Between Dimensions. Our ship hovers high above.

Duo explains, "We are once again in a Stealth Slot that keeps our presence invisible to the occupants," he points to a glow deep in the blackness of the Space-Between. "That is Daiyu at his Cosmos Comprehender."

Duo engages the trans-audio listening beam.

Katipo, a slender shapely female of Chinese-Lakota heritage with long silky black hair in a black form-fitting outfit that has a Latrodectus emblem on the chest enters and stands next to Daiyu. She is wearing Platinum Chota Transport Bracelets and has her Chota Invisibility Cloak in her hand.

With his eyes on the Comprehender Daiyu says, "We must get the Sacred Oglala Crest from Dimitri Talbot. You will go to the Raven on Planet Earth and promise him a better life with riches beyond his dreams."

"Do I need to RSR?"

"No. As an inhabitant of the Space-Between Dimensions, you cannot RSR. You may stay for short periods without generating any imbalance.

"How shall I present myself?"

"Use Meilin Bancroft-Qi's form while you are there."

"Do I take over her body?"

"No. Just shape-shift; you will have to visit Planet Theia and simulate Moonshadow Softwind as well. The plan is about deception. It is imperative that you gain both boys' confidence. You will need their help when we get the Crest."

"What shall I do when I get the Crest?"

"Bring it to me," the Black Jade responds, "The Sacred Oglala Crest has great powers, and must be used in the presence of the saddle with the horse, 'Runs like the Wind'."

Daiyu has not learned the total power of the Crest and how it is used with the Tome of Legends to decipher the all-powerful Chronicle of Unchangeable Changes.

"When the horse is a statue the boy uses his Transfer Ring to make him alive. Can I change him with my Chota Transport Bracelets?"

"Your bracelets have many powers, but not to change the horse. There is something else."

Daiyu reaches into his pocket and produces a Magical Transfer Ring with a Black Jade stone inscribed with a Latrodectus symbol and surrounded by ancient writings, and a small red diamond.

He hands the ring to Katipo, then draws it back, "I have been waiting for the appropriate time to have you use this," he hands her the ring, "place it on the first finger of your right hand when you are on Planet Earth. The red diamond must point to the end of your finger."

"Left hand when I am on Planet Theia?"

"Yes. This Magical Transfer Ring can only be used with the same language as the boys use on Planet Earth and Planet Theia. The incantations are within in the Tome of Legends and Chronicle of Unchangeable Changes. The ring will give you access to them. You will use your Abstract Data Recorder to download the access codes from my Cosmos Comprehender."

"How do I connect the Crest and the Tome of Legends if it is with the horse's saddle?"

"You must learn from the Chosen One. When you shapeshift as his mother you will convince him you are there to help. He will listen to his mother."

"I understand. When do I go?"

"Now."

Katipo faces the Comprehender, pushes keys on her belt buckle as rays shoot from the Comprehender to her Abstract Data Recorder Belt Buckle (ADR) downloading the codes. She stretches her arms out in front and clicks her Platinum Chota Transfer Bracelets together. She cries out to the Universe in her hybrid Chikota language. An energy field broadcasts radiant circles. She raises her arms and zooms up and away toward Earth in trans-travel mode landing near the old Qi barn as Meilin and Phir drive off in their SUV.

* * * * * * *

In response to a motion from Solo, Duo repositions our Spacecraft to another stealth slot where Anon and the Grey Forms are screening their Comprehender.

Anon looks up from the Comprehender, "There is another imbalance factor."

The Grey Forms are standing in their prescribed position next to Anon. The Male Grey Form bows and asks, "What has happened Immortal Unknown?"

"More Theialians have traveled to Earth. The task for the Chosen One has been expanded." Anon motions for the Male Grey Form to stand up straight, "There is more. Daiyu is sending Katipo to Planet Earth. The Presence will not be pleased that the outcast Black Jade plans to acquire the Sacred Crest for himself."

The Female Grey Form bows and asks, "Will the Thunder Beings be allowed to help now that the situation has developed to a greater disproportion?"

Anon motions for the Female Grey Form to stand up straight, "The Presence has agreed to a call for the Thunder Beings intersession, but only if they are called to assist the Chosen One."

Anon looks to the Grey Forms, "Prepare to visit Planet Earth. Take human shape, search out Katipo, and create a deception; do not reveal your identity. Be vigilant and remember you are there to help the boys. I will instruct Nous to beckon the Thunder Beings to assist when they are called by the Chosen One."

The Grey Forms bow, step backwards and slowly dematerialize as they trans-travel to Earth.

* * * * * * *

Solo repositions our spacecraft. Off our starboard side, there is the transparent duplicate of our spacecraft with our replicated forms inside. Duo waves his hands in a structured pattern over the Universal Portal Prompter. We see the duplicate of our Starcruiser move slowly toward the Planet Theia as we turn toward Earth.

Suddenly there is soul-wrenching awareness of a synchronistic happening as both Starcruisers snap into hyperdrive and rocket in opposite directions. We feel disembodied as a part of us goes in another direction. In an instant, we are landing on planet Earth as we did before, but now we are on Theia simultaneously. It is an extraordinary surreal sensation. The XR restraints release and we instinctively stand as our Starcruiser dematerializes leaving us in a fluid state.

As we set our feet on Earth, we see Gray Wolf and his cohorts leaving the old barn crouching low as they sneak over to the stable. They steal some horses leading them away to the cover of the forest edge before mounting. As it happens, they are spotted by one of the farm hands who calls Nigel on his mobile phone.

Nigel responds, "Gather the hands and meet me at the corral."

We turn the other way and see Katipo land near the Qi Farm House.

Katipo displaces herself to the Qi kitchen shape shifting into Meilin as Anza runs in.

"Hey mom, where's Yeye?"

Katipo, masquerading as Meilin responds, "He just went into town. What are you up to?"

"He was going to give me some lessons."

"What lessons?"

Katipo-Meilin doesn't wait for an answer, "Come with me," she takes Anza's hand and leads him out of the kitchen to the Grand Room.

"You and your grandfather come in here and then disappear through the wall to the Chamber Obscura. Show me how you go there."

"What do you mean?"

"I know about your secret room and what you do there," she pauses looking down at Anza, "show me."

Katipo-Meilin tugs at Anza's arm, but Anza resists.

"I can only go in with Yeye."

Katipo-Meilin looks at Anza with disgust, "Ok, we'll wait for your grandfather. There's something else. Let's go to the old barn. I know you're hiding the statue of a horse from the other planet," she takes Anza's hand and pulls him out of the house to the old barn.

Katipo-Meilin looks around the barn, as Anza stands quietly, "Here it is, the bronze statue," she turns to Anza, "you know where the Raven put the Crest that belongs with the saddle. Tell me."

"What raven? What crest?"

"The Raven and the Sacred Oglala Crest that came here with the statue," she grabs and shakes Anza by his shoulders and goes on with her interrogation, "tell me," frustrated, she continues, "go to your room. We'll see about this when your grandfather returns home."

Anza runs out of the barn. Katipo-Meilin inspects the statue's saddle, feeling the indentation left by the missing Crest. The Raven flies down and perches on a hay bale in full sight of Katipo-Meilin.

She speaks to the bird, "Hello Dimitri. What did you do with the Sacred Crest?"

"You're not his mother, are you?"

"I know you have the Crest ... I have come from the fourth dimension to offer you a reward and help you return to your home on Theia."

"Who sent you?"

"It doesn't matter ... I am here to help you ... help you do something you cannot do as a bird."

"I can change to my human self any time I want."

"I know you can change ... but, only for a moment, and then ---"

"It's Daiyu, isn't it? He sent you. I know he was exiled from Anon to the Space-Between Dimensions. I know he wants to control the balance of the planets, and believes the Oglala Crest holds the power."

"Like I said ... I know you can only be in your human form for a short time ... February 29th is close at hand ... you will run out of time and the planets will be destroyed ... you will be destroyed with them."

"And you too."

"No. I live in the Space-Between Dimensions. I will not be affected." She lies.

"What do you offer?"

"You lied to Gray Wolf about a promise made to you, but you must know that he does not have the power to grant such riches and the love of a beautiful woman."

"And you do?"

"Yes, plus political stature in your community."

"Well then ... let me think."

"Don't think too long."

* * * * * * *

Nigel and his men spot Gray Wolf and his men setting up camp in the tree outcropping near the base of the hills a short distance from the farmhouse. Knowing the lay of the land, they position themselves leaving the intruders no way out, or so they surmise. They wait until dark and make their move.

In the meantime, the Theialian intruders adapt to their surroundings easily since they are similar to what they are accustomed to on Planet Theia. A seasoned scout and trapper, Back Elk takes charge and secures the perimeter.

Nigel and his men have the tables turned on them as they attempt to capture the horse thieves. The cunning Lakota Indians surprise and capture Nigel and his men without a shot.

It takes most of the night, but Gray Wolf succeeds in convincing Nigel about their mission. They agree to team up and get the Sacred Oglala Crest.

Chapter Seven

A Call for Help

Anza stops running from the barn for a moment to see if his mother is following. Satisfied, he turns away and runs toward the Path of Knowledge. Upon arriving, he stops, looks around and calls out, "I need help."

The Path transforms with the face speaking, "What knowledge do you seek?"

"My mom has gone weird. Like, she isn't my mother"

"I can only help with knowledge. You need serious help." The Face in the Path turns away, "Watch, there above the meadow."

Anza looks to the sky and sees the Stellar Bubble Craft coming toward him faster than rocket speed stopping about two feet above the ground. Nous floats out of the craft suspended above the ground, encased in its normal glow, as the craft speeds away and disappears into outer space. "You can summon me yourself. Anytime, any place. What is troubling you child?"

"You call me child and you want me to save the world; my mother has gone weird on me," he pauses and continues sarcastically, "I am not a child, I am the Chosen One."

"Not a child. Hmm. Before we speak of your mother, you need to know why you are the Chosen One." Nous points to the face in the Path of Knowledge.

The Path speaks, "Your ancestor Tai Si, from the State of Qi, a descendant of Yu the Great, was selected by the Immortal Unknown to safeguard the Cosmic Eye Medallion and the secret of the Sacred Oglala Crest. Reincarnated at the beginning of the Xia Dynasty; she continued her destiny by way of the Peaches of Immortality and speaks through me.

Nous moves to watch Anza's reaction.

The Path continues, "Legend says King Wen of Zhou, was walking along the Wei River when he saw Tai Si and thought she was an angel or goddess and built a bridge of boats across the River to form a path to her. The path became her source of knowledge, and continues here today in a different form to help you. Tai Si married the King and had eight sons. You are the descendant of their son King Wu, and the Chosen One to safeguard the ancient secrets."

Anza looks at Nous and shouts out, "Wow."

Nous speaks, "You need to know about your mother's actions. Meilin is a kind and gentle person."

"Not today, she's different."

Nous looks at Anza, but does not speak.

"What am I to do? She said she knows about the Chamber Obscura, and can read the Tome of Legends, and, and the statue and the Crest, and the raven, and, and … Yeye told me that only he and me … I … me … can … oh," frustrated, he looks away, "mom is not supposed to know."

"This is serious. Do not be afraid. What I tell you next is going to be confusing." Nous looks sympathetically at Anza. "Your mother went into town with your grandfather a little while ago. What you saw was Katipo from the Space-Between Dimensions. Daiyu sent her to get the Sacred Oglala Crest. She can make herself look like your mother. It's called shape-shifting"

"Katipo is from where, and who is Daiyu?"

"Daiyu is the Black Jade," Anza listens to the story that finishes with, "... Katipo will be wearing a Magical Transfer Ring that looks almost like your ring. You must not reveal you know who she is."

"Holy sh ... shit ... sorry. She knows that I go to the Chamber Obscura, and I'm learning to read the Tome ... Chronicle ... oh you know. She'll probably find out that I can make the horse come alive."

"You have done that?" Nous pauses, "of course, you have. However, this exercise by Daiyu and Katipo requires a power, which I cannot use on Earth without permission. Phir Qi has the power, but you are the Chosen One," Nous hesitates, "have your grandfather summon me when he returns. You will need help from the Thunder Beings to accomplish your task."

"Yeye said they have powerful magic."

"I sense you mother and grandfather returning. Remember what I said."

"But, I don't have much time to save ---," Anza becomes silent as the Stellar Bubble Craft appears in the distant sky, swoops in, encompasses Nous, and flies off into outer space.

The confused Anza walks slowly away from the Path of Knowledge and sees his mother's SUV going down the road toward the house. "A lotta help you are," he admonishes the Path and runs home directly into the kitchen where Meilin and Phir are unpacking grocery bags.

"Hey mom! Hey Yeye!"

Meilin snaps back with, "Whatever happened to hello or hi? There are more groceries in the car. You can help bring them in."

Anza checks out his mother's hand for the ring. Not seeing it, he runs out and returns putting bags on the table. He runs out again returning with more groceries.

Phir smiles with a question, "Any more bags?"

"Nope, that's it."

The sound of hoof beats echoes through the window. "I hear the cuz coming. See ya."

Anza runs out as Qingling, Arthur and Longwei rein in with dust in their wake.

Meilin shouts out the window, "Be home in time to groom your horses before dinner."

Anza mounts his horse, "Come on, hyah-hyah," he shouts, and they ride off to the countryside. Anza leads the way and after a short ride, they rein in and dismount at the edge of the Path of Knowledge.

"You guys have to help me."

Qingling is quick to respond, "Not that save the world stuff again."

"Yes. Mom isn't always mom, and the raven took a Crest from the horse statue that we gotta get back to the other world so we don't ---"

"Whoa cuz," hollers Longwei, "we're just kids. Saving the world is for soldiers, and politicians or ---"

"Come on Longster, hear me out."

The kids sit alongside the Path of Knowledge ... time passes as Anza tells his story. He finishes with, "It's starting to get dark. You guys are sleeping over, so we can finish after dinner when Mom, Dad and Yeye go to bed. Meet me in my room and be quiet."

The kids mount their horses and ride back to the Qi Farm. They dismount and walk their horses to the stable where they groom them before dinner.

Later that night the kids sneak into Anza's room. Sitting cross-legged on Anza's bed, they stare at the antique bow propped up against the dresser.

Anza senses their interest, "I'll show you guys the bow later, but let's do this first."

Anza puts on his Magical Transfer Ring and takes the Oracle Frame from his bedside table. He taps the Oracle Frame with his ring finger swiping it around as symbols appear. He taps an icon and Xandr appears on the screen.

"Hi Anza. Who's that with you?"

The cousins sit with their mouths open in amazement.

"These are my cuz … cousins," they wave as he calls their names, "Qingling, Andrew and Longster. His name is really Longwei, but we call him Longster."

"My cousins are here too," Yellow Flower, Little Bear, and Payta appear and wave as he introduces his cousins. "We have to be quiet so's my folks don't hear"

"Do you know about Katipo?" Anza asks.

"Yes, she appeared as my Huku, and tried to get me to let her in the Chamber Obscura."

"Huku?" asks Arthur.

"Sorry. My mother," Xandr looks down with an almost shy pause, "I didn't let her in or tell her anything. What does she want from me?"

"She wants the Sacred Oglala Crest."

"Doesn't she know it's on your planet?"

"I guess she's covering all the bases."

"Bases, what are bases?"

"Never mind. I guess she figures if I don't tell, that you might."

"She's wasting her time 'cause I don't have a clue. Oh oh, gotta go."

"See ya," Anza presses the screen and it goes blank.

"Can you get MTV on that?" Longwei asks.

Anza jumps off the bed and goes to the dresser. He picks up the bow. Looking very superior, he whispers some unintelligible words and rises up sailing over and above the bed where he eases down and sits. The kid's eyes are as big as saucers.

"There are many things I can do with this magic, but I still need your help."

Qingling starts to speak, but Anza puts a finger to her lips to quiet her and slides off the bed putting the bow back by the dresser.

"It's time to go. We can talk tomorrow." Anza nudges the awestruck kids who slide off the bed and sneak out the door.

* * * * * * *

The next morning Anza and his cousins are walking along the Path of Knowledge when they encounter the human looking Grey Forms. They look at each other in wonderment. The Grey Forms materialize with human looks and proportions, but are still seven feet tall and grey in color.

Qingling looks at Anza, "Are they supposed to know about this place?"

Anza shrugs his shoulders, "I don't know."

The Male Grey Form smiles, "Good morning. It's a lovely day."

Anza steps forward a little, "How do you know about this place?"

The Female Grey Form responds with a smile, "We have been sent by Anon, the Immortal Unknown and are here to assist you."

Anza looks over at the Female Grey Form, "Are you Thunder Beings?"

"No. They are a last recourse. We just want you to know we are here to help," she looks down at the children stopping to fix her eyes on Anza, "The Chosen One can summon us with the Sacred Oglala Bow. Just ask for Grey Forms."

The Grey Forms rise up, change to fluid forms and slowly disappear.

Longwei still looking to the sky in amazement, "Who and what was that?"

Qingling turns to Anza with her eyes bugged out, "They're our helpers to save the world, right?"

"That's what they said."

"Soooo, just how do they help?"

Two raccoons show up on the Path. Notso sings out, "Hi kids. I saw you talking to the Greys. You shouldn't pay any attention to them."

"Which one are you?" asks Qingling.

Metoo twirls around, "He's Notso."

Anza glares at Notso, "I'm not supposed to pay heed to you. Besides, why shouldn't we listen to them?"

"I am more powerful and ..." Notso positions itself like a bull ready for the charge, pawing the ground. He morphs into a huge ten-foot-tall Gnashing Teeth Black Raccoon Monster and growls at Anza, "I am the one that can help."

The cousins jump back in fear, but Anza isn't duped by the raccoon's tomfoolery.

"Give me a break," he turns to Metoo as Notso becomes withdrawn and returns to normal size. "Do you know who they are?"

"They are the Grey Forms, the Immortal Unknown's assistants, and they only come when there is trouble. They don't actually do anything ... they report back, and he has Nous send the Thunder Beings."

Arthur looks at Metoo, "Who are the Thunder Beings, what do they have to do with us, and why should we believe a raccoon?"

"You can believe me. The Thunder Beings are very powerful and they will help you when the time is right."

* * * * * * *

Phir Qi is standing by the kitchen table as the kids run in almost knocking Meilin over as she was going out of the house to call them.

"You children must have built-in lunch meters, your mother was ---"

"I must feed the animals," Meilin calls out as she recovers from the teenage rampage and continues to the stables.

Anza is the first to speak. "Yeye, Yeye."

"I know, I know. Let's have lunch and talk. Sit."

The kids sit at the kitchen table and eat their lunch.

Phir looks around the table stopping at Anza, "What have you told them?" he points to the others.

"We've talked about the raven and the statue, and the Crest and the Thunder Beings, and ... and they've seen the Oracle Frame and the Greys and the Raccoons and ... and Xandr and Theia and ---"

"Oh, my," he gets up from the table and makes a grandfatherly gesture for the kids to continue eating. Pacing, he stops from time to time, and paces some more.

"Yeye. Who are the Thunder Beings?"

Phir pours a cup of tea and sits with the kids. Everyone eats in silence. After lunch he commands the cousins in a soft but firm way, "You best be getting on home."

The cousins run out as Phir looks at Anza, "We have much to do. Get your backpack ready with your magical things and we will be off at first light."

"Why not now? I have to save the world, ya know."

"Tomorrow is soon enough. Your school work needs to be done ... now."

* * * * * * *

The sun is coming up over the meadow, the air is crisp and the grass glistens with the morning dew as Phir Qi and Anza walk along the Path of Knowledge. They stop at the colorful pink-leaf Sugi tree. Phir takes off his dragon shawl and spreads it under the Sacred Chinese Cedar. Anza removes his backpack and they sit.

Within moments, the Grey Forms appear as fluid forms near the end of the Path manifesting into humans as they walk toward them.

The Male Grey Form looks down, "Good morning," he acknowledges Phir with a nod.

Anza stands, "Hello. We have come here looking for answers … how to find the Crest, save the world. Ya know. Simple every day stuff."

The Female Grey Form is quick to react, "We do not have answers. You can get knowledge from the Path."

"We need help. What about the Thunder Beings, or Nous?"

The Male Grey Form speaks, "We cannot call for the Thunder Beings, but we can direct you … only Anon, the Immortal Unknown, can release them. You can summon Nous for help."

The Greys rise up becoming fluid forms and slowly disappear.

Phir stands, "It is time to summon Nous."

"But … I ---"

"It must be done."

Anza looks up and turns around with his arms stretching up to the sky, "Nous … Nous."

The Stellar Bubble Craft appears instantly leaving Nous floating above the ground, and disappearing into outer space as it did previously.

"Good morning child," Nous looks briefly at Phir, "it is good to see you again, I enjoyed our talk the other day," with eyes back to Anza, "you summoned me."

"I must find the Sacred Crest."

"Use all that is available to you. Look down and ask the Path of knowledge for information."

Anza looks down as the face appears in the Path. "What am I to do next?"

The Path speaks, "Go to the Chamber Obscura and call for the Chronicle of Unchangeable Changes using your Magical Transfer Ring with the Tome of Legends. Xandr will help search for the secret code that allows you to use the magic of the Oglala. Download the information to your Oracle Frame. Use the Sacred Oglala Crest's counterpart, the Cosmic Eye Medallion, to interpret the code. It will lead you to the place where you will find the Sacred Oglala Crest."

"The Cosmic Eye Medallion?"

"It is in the crystal podium; you will instinctively know how to use it. Go now, time is drawing nigh."

Nous gestures and is rocketed away in the Stellar Bubble Craft.

Chapter Eight

The Sacred Oglala Crest

Anza and Phir walk back home in silence. Anza sits nervously at the kitchen table eating his lunch as Phir places a cup of Chinese herbal tea on the table and sits next to Anza.

"Drink this, Sūnzi. It will calm you for the task at hand."

Anza drinks the tea, "Yeye, you have to help me with all this Oglala and Medallion stuff."

"You must go alone."

"But ---"

Phir stands, gives Anza a kiss on the forehead, steps back with a stern look and points for Anza to go.

Anza goes to the Grand Room stopping at the place of the Invisible Wall. He waves his arm and incants in Chinese, "Dakai ménhù." The wall in front of him becomes transparent, and the Chamber Obscura appears. Anza cautiously goes through the wall.

The Raven is at the window watching as Anza disappears through the wall.

Anza stands at the podium and points his ring finger. The Tome of Legends glows with the pages turning. He concentrates and goes into a trance as the pages stop turning and become still.

Xandr's voice comes from the Tome of Legends, "I am here Anza."

"I must have the secret code of the Oglala so I can find the Sacred Crest."

Anza looks down at the Tome accidentally waving his hand, and the pages begin turning again.

Xandr says, "I'll look as soon as the pages stop turning," there's a pause, "okay, they stopped; this must be it," he jumps back, "whoa, it's sending sparks to my Magical Picture Frame." The sparking stops, "What do I do now?"

"Point your ring at the Picture Frame."

Xandr waves his ring finger over the Magical Picture Frame; it becomes brighter as the code projects from the Chronicle of Unchangeable Changes to the Magical Picture Frame within a three-dimensional laser beam. After a moment, the code transfer is complete. The Magical Picture Frame's glow diminishes, and the code is on its way to Earth and the Tome of Legends with a soft zap.

Anza lowers his hand, picks up the Magical Oracle Frame as laser rays shoot from the Tome of Legends to the Oracle's screen. Anza sees the three-dimensional secret code on the screen as it downloads.

The Cosmic Eye Medallion pulsates as it radiates in the Crystal Glass Podium. Anza points his ring and the Cosmic Eye Medallion moves out of the Podium into his hand. He moves the nine sided Medallion over the secret code and nothing happens. He transfers the Medallion to his left hand and points his Magical Transfer Ring at the Oracle Frame.

The concave variegated blue-translucent-crystal-enneagon has a cosmic eye symbol offset from the middle toward the top & centered on the second angle point. The eye becomes a magnifier; focusing on a three-dimensional map that has directions to where the Raven has hidden the Sacred Crest.

The bright-eyed Anza tilts the Oracle Frame, and the location of the Sacred Oglala Crest pulsates in a brilliant purple color, moving out to the surface of the screen. The map zooms in as a holographic view of a cave opening in the side of the mountain.

Anza leaves the Chamber Obscura, puts on his cool sunglasses on and heads to the old barn where he spots a woman in the shadows, ignoring her as he passes.

The woman is Katipo wearing a blouse, blue jeans with matching jacket, boots and a western style hat. She sets out to follow Anza, but is intercepted by two Grey Forms clad in dark clothes, masquerading as humans and carrying bibles.

The Female Grey Form says, "Good afternoon sister. We have not seen you here before. Are you new to these parts?"

"I'm ... I am visiting my family, the Qi's," she lies.

"We are from," she points, "over there. We are here to visit Meilin Bancroft-Qi. Come join us."

Anza creeps slowly as the afternoon sunlight shines through the cracks in the old barn roof creating an eerie and magical light across the bronze statue. He grabs his backpack, "Want to go for a ride?" he asks it as he points his ring finger at him chanting, "Lái shēnghuó."

'Runs like the Wind' comes to life. Anza jumps on a hay bale, mounts him and they race out of the old barn down the road toward the cave shown on the map.

Katipo becomes agitated as 'Runs like the Wind' gallops by with Anza on his back. "I ... I ---."

"That is Anza; always riding off ... he will be back soon. Come into the house," the Male Grey Form orders while grabbing her arm.

Having followed Anza to the old barn the Raven realizes he has discovered the location of the Crest and is going to get it. Knowing he will need some help, he flies off to where Gray Wolf, Nigel, and their band of outlaws are hanging out.

He swoops down to their camp, and morphs into Dimitri Talbot, "The boy is riding off to get the Crest, and I know where he is going."

"Let's go," commands Gray Wolf.

"Remember your promise."

"Of course," Gray Wolf responds as he smiles at Nigel and the others, "of course."

Dimitri morphs back to the Raven and flies away leading the way to the cave.

* * * * * * *

Anza reins in for a brief moment and checks the Oracle Frame. He returns it to his backpack and gently urges 'Runs like the Wind' with his heels into his side. He starts in a slow gallop, increasing his gait and soon is running at a speed to match his name.

The Oracle Fame emits a loud sound indicating they have arrived at the entrance to the cave shown on the map as the winter sun begins its early descent behind the hills. Anza reins in, removes his sunglasses and dismounts leaving his horse ground tied.

Taking a flashlight from his backpack, he goes into the cave. It is damp, cold and dark, but not silent. He looks up, down and all around. The light beam spots a lot of bats making weird squeaking noises and hanging in the crevices. The bats are spooked and begin flying around crashing into Anza. Momentarily scared he jumps aside, takes a deep breath and composes himself. The bat colony soon goes back to cluster in their roost. Anza waits a few moments and moves guardedly deeper into the uninviting cave.

He stops and takes the Oracle Frame from his backpack. He moves his finger across the multitude of icons until a bright blue beam shoots out; first straight, then curving from side to side, then up and down. With a *zap,* it locks in on a crevice high in the wall.

He shines his flashlight on the jagged but climbable slope. Up he goes like an amateur rock climber, slipping and almost falling, finally reaching a deep crevice where the Raven hid the Sacred Oglala Crest. He removes the Crest, puts it in his backpack, retreats down the slope and runs out of the cave to the waiting horse.

Anza is unable to mount huge steed without help, and motions for him to bow down on one knee. Grabbing the pommel of the white saddle, he sets his foot in the stirrup and swings aboard while the stallion instinctively stands erect. An accomplished rider, he urges him to leave with a neck rein and a slight forward shifting of weight.

Satisfied with his finding, he rides down the dirt road at wind speed. But, with the evening light casting shadows across his path he slows his horse to a canter upon approaching a sharp turn.

Laying-in-wait ready to ambush the unsuspecting boy are Nigel and his men, and their new partners-in-crime Gray Wolf and his band of Indians. They jump out from the cover of the trees frightening him and his horse.

The mighty stallion spooked by the disruption comes to sudden stop and rears to his hind legs, throwing Anza from the saddle despite his desperate attempts to stay mounted. As he goes down, he instinctively rolls away from the animal's dangerous hooves, but is knocked unconscious as his head slams into a rock alongside the road. 'Runs like the Wind' settles down.

Nigel searches Anza's backpack and almost immediately finds the Crest, "Let's get outta here."

"What about him?" asks one of the bad guys.

"Leave him. I've got what we came for."

The bad guys ride off, leaving the injured Anza.

The Raven flies above keeping an eye on Gray Wolf and the treasure.

'Runs like the Wind' walks to Anza and nudges him with his head. Getting no reaction, he tries again, and again. He waits; apprehensive and nervous he paws the ground. Time passes; he looks around and gallops away.

* * * * * * *

The Grey Forms have a squirming Katipo confined and uncomfortable with their continuous bible readings.

"Excuse me," Katipo pleads as she gets up and heads for the Great Room.

"You can not leave, we have just begun," cries the Female Grey Form.

"I'll be right back," Katipo lies.

She goes to the Great Room and waves her arms as she remembered Anza doing, she chants, "Dakai ménhu." The wall becomes transparent and the triumphant Katipo goes through wall into the Chamber Obscura.

She goes directly to the podium, reaches into her pocket and places the Magical Transfer Ring on her finger. Noticing it is backwards, she removes it and puts it back on and points at the Tome of Legends. The pages begin to glow and turn.

Katipo pushes buttons on her Abstract Data Recorder Belt Buckle. A red beam streams and combines with her Transfer Ring beam. The words and images of the code bounce around and finally flash on a holographic screen above the Podium. In a moment, a three-dimensional image of the map that Anza saw moments ago lingers above the Tome of Legends. She downloads it to her ADR, smiles and leaves passing the Grey Forms as she goes out through the kitchen.

Self-satisfied she says, "Later," continuing passed the table and out the door.

Katipo rushes down the dirt road just moments after Nigel and Gray Wolf and their band of outlaws gallop away in the opposite direction. 'Runs like the Wind' races by as she comes upon Anza lying unconscious. She looks in the backpack lying next to him. There is no Crest to be found. She checks Anza's pulse and the bruise on his head, "Sorry kid. I gotta go."

She calmly raises her arms to the sky; slowly lowering them to her toes changing into her Latrodectus outfit. She stretches her arms out in front, looks back at Anza and clicks her bracelets together. Radiant circles form as she zooms up and away returning to the Space-Between Dimensions as 'Runs like the Wind' returns to the old barn and walks slowly inside.

Daiyu turns to face Katipo as she returns to his side crying out, "Nigel Churchill and Gray Wolf have the Crest."

* * * * * * *

We return our sights to the Stellar Monitor. Our vision focuses on Nous in the Province of Acceptance and on Earth simultaneously.

Nous sees Katipo fly away, focuses on Earth below and spots Anza on the dirt road, summons the Stellar Bubble

Craft and zooms to Anza. The Craft disappears leaving Nous floating above the ground encased in light. Nous extends a hand pointing a finger at Anza. A Green Ray shines on Anza's forehead moving from side to side; a few moments pass, Nous smiles as the Green Ray completes its healing magic. Miraculously all signs of his injury are removed.

Anza awakens rubbing his head, "What happened?"

"You have fallen from 'Runs like the Wind'," Nous says with a stern child-like look, "You should not be riding him. Grey Wolf and his band have taken the Crest from your backpack and ---"

Anza cuts Nous short, "I must ---"

"You must learn the *way* first."

"But, we don't have time."

"Time is an elusive concept, little Tian yì. It is the Presence's way of making you believe everything does not happen at once. Once you learn Paesre, which will bring the past, present and future in concert ... you will be able to achieve your task as the Chosen One."

"Yeye told me that, but I don't know how."

"You and Xandr must travel to the four-dimensional world and learn the way." Nous looks for a reaction, but Anza is still dazed, "You will use the Sacred Oglala Bow and Xandr will use the Waluta Cane for your Trans-Dimensional Travel. Do you understand?"

"We're gonna fly, right?"

Nous looks down and smiles.

"So how will we ---?"

Nous interrupts, "You will trans-travel through the Portal of Ojas. Enough for today child; go home; your parents will be worried. You have much to learn. Rest tonight, I will see you tomorrow."

Anza watches the Stellar Bubble Craft return for Nous and disappear into the starlit evening sky. He walks home getting there in time for dinner.

After dinner, Meilin and Baxter get up from the table, "We're going to watch TV. What are you two up to?" Baxter asks.

Phir chimes in, "I'm going to read, and Anza has studies."

When his parents are out of range, Anza looks at his grandfather, "Something happened today Yeye."

"I know Sūnzi, I know."

"I gotta get it back."

"First, you must learn the *way*."

"That's what Nous said. Something about a place called Ojas."

"It is more than a place. It is a container; a celestial service station with all the cosmic energy you will need to travel to the four-dimensional world of Anon; it is also the gateway between the spiritual and the material. It is Paesre."

"When will I know more?"

"You will waken in the night. I will be in the old barn. We will continue the journey to your destiny."

Anza awakens from a nightmare where the calendar shows February 28th and the Earth is beginning to shake. He dresses, grabs his MTR and quietly slips out of the house and into the old barn where Phir is waiting.

"Yeye, I had a terrible dream."

"What was so terrible?"

"I saw that we had just one day left."

"That would be terrible. Let's get started."

Anza and Phir sit on the straw covered floor inside a Circle of Stones; a chill moves through the old barn and Anza watches silently as Phir lifts the Sacred Oglala Bow high up. He closes his eyes tilting his head back with an impulsive I Ching time travel chant. The Deer's Tail begins waving in the tranquil room, slowly at first, then fluttering as if a strong wind was blowing, but there was none. The moonlight that filtered through the cracks in the old barn frame soon dissipated leaving a 'quiet-before-the-storm' eerie feeling.

Moments seem like a lifetime until a great vibration followed by a series of thunderous claps shudder the old wooden framed barn. The barn creeks and feels like it should crumble to the ground. Suddenly the darkness becomes a soft glow that rapidly intensifies to a lightening bright illumination that fills the room accompanied by a small breeze that quickly turns into a force lifting and whisking them up and out the doorway as they transform to a fluid shape.

Simultaneously in the Stellar Monitor, we see Xandr and Emera sitting within the Sacred Hoop. Emera raises his Cane, the Waluta unfurls. They are whisked-up and out of the stable in a mini tornado-like funnel on their way to the Portal of Ojas as they, too, transform to a fluid shape for trans-travel.

Chapter Nine
The Portal of Ojas

Solo and Duo work their magic to join our original and duplicate Spacecrafts as one ship for a new and amazing fight to the outskirts of the Residence of the Most High. We realize we have come together with our duplicates as we stop at the Portal of Ojas.

Phir and Anza ... Xandr and Emera arriving at exactly the same time from different directions approach the Portal of Ojas; a brilliant lavender shimmering circular object with a soft inviting white light in the center. Their fluid forms revert to human shapes.

A voice; heard as the Stellar Bubble Craft appears between them. Nous speaks, "You have arrived at the Portal of Ojas, the gateway to the Residence of the Most High; the fluid of life that connects the mind to the body and consciousness. Follow me."

The Stellar Bubble Craft moves slowly as the Synchro Gateway appears and expands just enough for it to clear the Portal closing behind as it passes.

Phir and Emera raise their Bow and Cane at the same time while the boys enjoy this exciting new adventure. The Synchro Gateway appears again, expanding just enough and gently lifting the boys and their grandfathers inside the Ethereal Cortex.

They continue their trans-dimensional journey through vibrations, angelic music and ever-changing rainbows to the massive entrance of the Residence of the Most High where they stop and wait.

Magnetically drawn into a cavalcade with the Stellar Bubble Craft; our Starcruiser slows down hovering somewhere and everywhere at the same moment at the inner edge of the Portal of Ojas with front row seats to an extraordinary happening. We stop abruptly as an invisible force just inside the Portal restricts our flight. We cannot enter into the Ethereal Cortex, but are able to see and hear the happenings by way of our Stellar Monitor.

One of us asks, "Why don't we go further?"

"You are not allowed," responds a gentle voice from within.

"But we were there before."

"That was a digital illusion of a reality to demonstrate the existence of the Ultimate Unknown; a contrivance to assist your decision to RSR. Only invited guests may pass beyond this point of the Portal of Ojas. You may observe in your Stellar Monitor."

The Immortal Unknown stands with his back to us watching the Cosmos Comprehender. Two Translucent Grey Forms stand at his left. The image on the massive Comprehender screen zooms in on Anza, Phir, Xandr and Emera as they fly through the Portal of Ojas. There is an instantaneous, but momentary zoom-in image of our Starcruiser snapping back to an image of the Stellar Bubble Craft that becomes center screen.

A soft but authoritarian voice comes from all directions at once, "Prepare for our guests."

The Grey Forms turn and sail upright a little above the non-existent floor to the massive pair of crystal doors. Anon waves His hand and the wall opens with a deep sigh as the Grey Forms welcome the boys and their grandfathers cautioning them to be silent as they walk on the imaginary floor.

The Stellar Bubble Craft sails between the Grey Forms stopping somewhere in the distance.

The Male Grey Form summons the guests, "Please follow. Do not speak until asked."

Anza, Phir, Xandr and Emera walk gingerly behind the Grey Form continuing toward the Immortal Unknown.

Anza whispers, "Is this God?"

The Female Grey Form stops and turns to Anza, "No, It is Anon, The Immortal Unknown. You must not speak unless you are asked."

They stop a few feet short. The Grey Forms move to Anon's left. There is stillness for what seems like an eternity until heavenly music fills the space and the boys respond with a breath of relief, as they seem to be in concert with the breathing of the space they occupy. Anza and Xandr look at each other. Xandr makes a small waist-high wave. Anza smiles, Phir and Emera tug on the boys' arms.

The Stellar Bubble Craft stops two feet above the transparent floor. Nous floats out of the Craft, which flies off slowly leaving Nous hovering and facing Anon's right side. The screen of the Cosmos Comprehender changes images. Nigel Churchill, Gray Wolf and their band of outlaws appear on the screen.

Nous speaks in a soft child-like voice, "They are planning to take the Crest back to Planet Theia and leave the horse on Planet Earth. They do not understand the consequences. This is most troublesome."

Anon turns facing his guests. The Grey forms move to his left side while Nous moves to his right. He puts his hands together in front about shoulder high and opens his arms to receive his guests; the heavenly music builds to a crescendo and stops.

"Welcome."

Phir and Emera bow, nudging the boys to do the same. Anza and Xandr look at each other, shrugging their shoulders and bow. Anon gestures. Everyone stands up straight.

"Nothing stimulates outrageous theories so effectively as an absence of evidence. The Crest alone does not have the power to ..." He turns to Nous, "Please explain to Tian yì and the others."

Nous moves partly in front of Anon, "The secrets of the Sacred Oglala Crest and the Cosmic Eye Medallion can only be energized by your Magical Transfer Rings. Katipo has a Magical Transfer Ring with the same power. However, only limited readings of the Tome of Legends and Chronicle of Unchangeable Changes are possible with the rings. You need more than the rings."

Nous looks at Anza, "You may speak now Tian yì."

"You called me that before; what does it mean?"

"It means, the Chosen One."

Xandr asks, "Am I chosen too?"

"You are like your counterpart Anza, but the Lakota do not have a chosen one."

"The bad guys have the Crest," Anza speaks with concern, "What do they want with it if they don't have the ring to activate the code?"

Nous recognizes the anxiety in Anza's voice and offers a condolence. "They do not know what other powers they must have to complete the unexplained and to change the unchangeable." Nous examines Anza's face to see if he understands, "the secrets required to energize the Oglala magic can only be carried out while in Paesre."

"What are the other powers? Katipo has a ring just like mine. Why doesn't she ---?"

Nous interrupts, "We have seen Katipo talking with the Raven. They will soon be seeking help from Carl Drinkwater and Nigel and anyone else they think will help find the Crest.

"Carl, but he's just ---"

"I will tell you who is conspiring to use the Crest, and I will instruct you in the use of your powers." Nous looks at Xandr, "You too have powers, but not like Anza."

Anza looks quizzically at Nous, "Why doesn't he," pointing at Anon, "wave his arms or something and take care of all of this?"

"The creator has given all humans free will. What has been done by humans has to be undone by humans." Nous looks at the boys, "You must team up in order to save both your worlds. It is time for your lessons. I will join you soon."

Nous turns for a blessing from the Immortal Unknown.

With the palms of his hands facing up, Anon raises his arms and slowly lowers them turning his palms downward while nodding his head.

Nous bows and turns around to meet the Stellar Bubble Craft, which has stopped two feet above the transparent floor. Nous moves inside, and the Craft slowly moves away.

The Grey Forms turn and sail upright a little above the floor to the massive pair of crystal doors signaling for the boys to follow.

Anza and Xandr trans-dimensionally travel to a place high atop a cloud covered mountain peak. A light breeze dissipates a portion of the clouds exposing a pathway to a multi colored crystal edifice.

Anza looks at the Grey Forms, "How did we get here so fast?"

"It is an advanced form of quantum teleportation," replies the Female Grey Form.

"What's that mean?" Xandr asks.

"Simply put, you got here by receiving our thoughts, and then you think of this place subconsciously. As you can see, those thoughts brought you here."

"We can fly ... uh; I mean we can travel to places like this just by thinking about it? How do both Anza and me ... I ... do that ... think about traveling to the same place at the same time?"

"You are counterparts with entangled protons that we sent to you. The protons perform a polarization measurement whose outcome links you together. Entanglement is a consequence of quantum mechanics as it relates to teleportation.

"Sorry I asked."

"In order to understand you must Paesre. Go inside. Nous will join you in a moment."

"What do we do now?" Xandr asks Anza.

"That Grey guy said we are linked together. So, let's point our rings and see if anything happens."

"Aren't you afraid?"

"What the worst that can happen? We get ourselves zapped back home. Ready... set ... point."

The boys point their Magical Transfer Rings at the mountain peak and the facets of the crystal surface vibrate creating a melodious movement. They stand in awe as the sparkling crystals separate creating a surprisingly soft and inviting opening.

"It works," Xandr exclaims, "now what?"

"We go inside. Come on," Anza leads the way.

The cloud-like doorway slowly closes behind them.

 The boys creep in and look around in wonderment. The walls, floor and ceiling appear to be made of a translucent cloud-like substance with the exterior crystal surface shining through. Celestial music is everywhere. Soft ambient light is constantly changing, white, green, light blue, lavender. Suddenly all restraints are magically removed and they start running here and there. They jump ... twirl, and laugh hysterically. They stop as quickly as they started and look at each other.

Xandr speaks first, "Where are we?"

"I don't know, heaven, maybe."

"We can't be in heaven. You have to be dead to go to heaven. Are we dead?"

"I don't think so. Nous said it's time for our lessons about Paesre."

"Why do I have to learn? You're the Chosen One."

"Don't know, but Nous said we must team-up," he grabs Xandr's arm. "What's it like in your world?"

The boys walk to a flower covered surreal platform. They sit on a stone bench that seems to be as soft as a feather bed.

They tell each other about their world. Anza finishes telling about Earth, "So we're almost the same."

"Yeah, but you've got all those new gadgets and stuff."

"You have the same stuff; they just look different."

Nous enters floating toward them stopping a short distance away.

Anza asks, "What is this place?"

"It is my home; the Province of Acceptance. This is where you will learn Paesre, and about your powers. It is time ..., *as you perceive it*. We will start with the powers of your Magical Transfer Rings. I will demonstrate some of what you can do as a team. Look there."

Nous extends a hand. A green ray from its finger shines on the floor, an opening appears with a holographic image of Carl Drinkwater and the Sheng Chi Master sitting under a Cedar Tree. We hear them talking.

"Why do we have to sit under this tree?" asks Carl.

"You do not have to sit here, but it is safe for me when I am here with you. The Crest you have stolen is from the other world, which has caused a big problem."

"What does that have to do with where I sit? Besides I had nothing to do with it coming here from the other world."

"The one that wrongfully has the Sacred Crest on this planet is subject to lightning strikes. This Cedar Tree, the Axis Mundi, can never be struck by lighting."

"There's not a cloud in the sky."

"It is said that the Thunder Beings can appear at any time to avenge a serious wrong doing."

"Never mind them old stories. Let's get on with it."

The Sheng Chi Master raises his arms and goes into a trance. Thunder blasts through the countryside with lightning striking everywhere, all around the Cedar Tree.

Carl looks scared, "What's happening?"

"It is the Thunder Beings."

Carl jumps when the lighting strikes close. He scrambles back as the old master lowers his arms.

"Did you call for the thunder and lighting old man?"

The Sheng Chi Master extends his arms comfortably with the palms of his hands facing upward as if to receive heavenly manna and smiles. "It is the way of the Thunder Beings."

Nous closes the holographic image and opening. The green ray disappears from his fingertip, "You have the same power when you are joined together. We will continue later. The Sheng Chi Master has deceived them. In due course, they will find out what he has done. We must hurry."

"What are we supposed to learn so we can save our planet?" the boys say in unison. Surprised they look at each other, then to Nous.

"You are experiencing the unity of your nature. We must go deeper into the Province of Acceptance."

Chapter Ten

Paesre

We see Anza, Xandr and Nous move away. Solo attempts to follow, but is reminded that our Spacecraft cannot pass beyond Ojas. However, we can hear the lesson Nous is teaching Anza and Xandr.

Anza and Xandr are deep in a place they will soon realize to be the essence of the Provence of Acceptance. They begin to experience each other in an unusual form; something outside their three-dimensional worlds. They appear the same, but strangely different. They seem to be in one place, then in another place at the same time. They instantly accept, without any trepidation, the weird and wonderful phenomenon.

Nous senses they have developed the ability to grasp a fourth dimension, "As three-dimensional beings, you perceive time only as a result of memory. If you had zero memory, you could not detect time and you would exist only for the moment."

"Will something happen to our memory, like we forget our family and friends?" asks Xandr.

"You will learn to exist as four-dimensional beings while you perform your task to save your planets. Time seems like a straight line going on forever to the three-dimensional being. As a four-dimensional being you can simply go from where you are to any other place while remaining *where you are* because you can perceive the fourth dimension."

Anza looks enlightened, "So, if I go from one spot to another, and I'm still in the same spot then I won't know I moved because I'm everywhere at once. Paesre?"

"Yes. Paesre is the past, present and future combined. In the three-dimensional state, you would consider time as infinite, but in the fourth dimension, it is finite. There is more, but you do not need to know all the quantum aspects to accomplish your task. Your family and friends will continue to be the same as before your transition between the third and fourth dimensions."

"When do we get started?" asks Xandr.

"You started when you transitioned Ojas and began your acceptance here in the Province; you are there and here simultaneously."

"Cool," the boys sing out in concert.

"We will begin the mental exercises necessary for you to Paesre at will."

"What do we do?" They ask in harmony as if they are one.

"Knowledge of the Conscientiousness of the Ages is foremost in your lesson today."

"Why is it important to know this before we learn about the trans-travel?"

"To know about conscientiousness is fundamental to what you will be doing, but to understand is necessary."

"Okay, so what is it all about?" Anza asks.

"Through the ages humans have survived through many difficult situations that required changes to what they thought to be unchangeable circumstances."

"What did they do?"

"Simply put; they became an orderly and industrious society with a sense of responsibility, self-control and they established social traditions."

"So survival is not the only driving force."

"That is correct, but in your task to save your world, you must use a certain amount of organization, persistence, control and motive. Now we will begin the meditation process so you will Paesre at will. Ready?"

"Yes," responds the synchronized boys.

Chapter Eleven

The Forest of Understanding

Anza and Xandr complete their acceptance of Paesre and the art of Trans-Dimensional Travel and are ready to be put to the test by Nous.

"Clear your minds of all memory," sensing their state, "good, now become one with the universe," a short pause and, "be on Planet Theia; at the Softwind Farm Stable."

Anza and Xandr stand quiet with their eyes closed and instinctively point their ring fingers toward Theia. A lavender glow surrounds them. They dematerialize and instantly find themselves materializing in the deep of the night in the Softwind farm stable. Astonished, they feel to see if they are real.

When Anza and Xandr dematerialized, they left a shadowy image of themselves as Solo turns our Spacecraft away from Ojas. There is an instantaneous power surge and we trans-dimensionally travel to Theia.

We get there as the boys materialize. *Our duplicates* remain until Phir and Emera transition to Earth and Theia simultaneously; then we will join our originals on Theia.

Anza looks around, "What is this place?"

"It's our stable; 'Runs like the Wind' used to stay here. This is where it all started when Tunksila put a spell on the stableboy, and sent him to your world. Will we get in trouble with both of us here at the same time?"

"Tunksila? Your grandfather?"

"Yes."

"Nous said when we Paesre and Trans-Dimensionally travel we are in harmony with the Universe."

"So-o-o, we're not gonna get in trouble. Right, oh Chosen One?"

"Right; don't call me that, we're in this together."

"Ok. So what's next?"

"Where do you go to understand what's happening?"

"The Forest of Understanding; let's go."

* * * * * * *

Phir and Emera are watching Anza and Xandr as they disappear. The Male Grey Form motions to them.

"You must return home."

Phir and Emera follow the Grey Forms to the Crystal Doors and stop when the Grey Forms turn back for approval. Anon gestures and the doors open. They follow the Grey Forms through the opening. The doors close behind them. The Female Grey Form puts her arms around Emera, and the Male Grey Form does the same with Phir. A gentle force surrounds them and they travel through a space-time continuum guided to Theia and Earth simultaneously with their Greys. Phir and the Male Grey Form arrive at the Qi Farmhouse. The Male Grey Form leaves Earth returning to his home. Emera and the Female Grey Form arrive next to the Softwind stable as Anza and Xandr run out. The Female Grey Form leaves Theia returning to her home.

"Boys, boys," shouts Emera Softwind as the Female Grey Form dematerializes.

The boys stop in their tracks.

Emera continues, "Tȟakóža. Where are you going?"

"I'm taking Anza to the Forest."

"You can go later. Your mother has supper ready."

"What about Anza?"

"He will eat with us."

"What about Huku and Ate?"

"They know you have a friend staying over."

Anza joins Xandr and his family for a traditional Lakota supper. The country kitchen is similar to Anza's Earthly home, but with antique looking furniture.

"I didn't know we had any Chinese families in these parts," says Xandr's mother, Moonshadow.

Emera jumps in, "He's new to the area."

"Any friend of our son is welcome. I understand you will be staying the night. Do your parents know you are here?"

"Yes ma'am."

"I will fix a cot in ---"

"He can stay in my room with me."

After supper, the boys go for a walk on the road to the Forest of Understanding when they hear a voice from behind. "Wait up," shouts Yellow Flower.

They turn to see Little Bear, Payta and Yellow Flower running after them.

"Oh, oh," Xandr looks concerned.

"Oh, oh what? Aren't they your cousins?"

"They can't go into the Forest with us."

"How come?"

"We have stuff to do, and they don't know about ---"

"Too late."

The cousins catch up, and Payta asks, "Where are you going?"

"Hi. Remember me?" Anza asks.

Little Bear jumps forward, "We saw you in Xandr's picture thing-a-ma-bob. You're from the other world. How'd you get here?"

"It's along story."

"We've got time."

"We have to go into the Forest."

"What forest? There's no forest around here."

Xandr points, "There. See there; that is the Forrest of Understanding. Come on Anza," he points at the others. "You gotta stay out here."

Yellow flower looks in amazement at the trees that seemed to appear out of nowhere, "Where'd they come from?"

Xandr looks at Anza. "Let's go." They run toward the forest edge with the cousins close behind. They come to a screeching halt at the entrance to the Forest of Understanding as two squirrels jump out from behind a tree.

Xandr looks down at them, "What do you guys want?"

Negi the evil squirrel looks up, "We're here to help."

"Which one are you?"

The other squirrel, Posi, speaks, "He's Negi."

"You're trouble, come on Anza."

The squirrels disappear. Anza and Xandr run into the forest with the cousins close behind.

An incredible wind howls behind them closing the entrance to the Forest of Understanding.

"What's happening?" asks a scared Little Bear.

"This has never happened before," replies Xandr. He looks at Anza. "Any ideas?"

"They haven't been here in the Forest."

"No, I mean yes they haven't."

The trees start to close in on them like something or someone is pushing from outside. They come closer and closer almost taking the air away. Then the oak and pine trees start raining acorns and pinecones. The kids are scared.

"What's next? Are we gonna die?" asks Payta.

Suddenly a massive pine tree starts shooting pine needles all around them.

Instinctively, Anza points his Magical Transfer Ring and creates a Floating Battle Shield that moves around at his silent command deflecting the attacking missiles.

"Everyone stand still," commands Anza. He looks around and sees three paths. He must make a choice. A narrow pathway covered with lavender colored leaves on the ground seems to beckon him. He points his Bow and the Pathway and it speaks, "Follow me."

They move slowly as the trees reach out grabbing at the cousins. Grabbed by an oak tree branch, Anza's Battle Shield becomes useless.

Anza commands, "Walk between Xandr and me. Stay close."

After what seems like an eternity, they come to a clearing. The acorn and pinecone bombardment stops, and the lavender leaves raise up forming a shield from the pine needle bullets.

A silver circle appears around the clearing at the bottom of the lavender shield. In the center is a single eighty foot tall Axis Mundi Cottonwood Tree where the squirrels are waiting.

Posi calls out, "Come here, under the Safe Tree."

The kids run to the cover of the Cottonwood.

Posi points up through a small opening in the trees, "Look."

The Stellar Bubble Craft swoops down through the opening and hovers as Nous gets out. The Craft speeds away as Nous floats above the ground. The cousins gasp in bewilderment.

The dazed Yellow Flower asks, "What ... who?"

"It's Nous," answers Xandr, "I'll tell you later."

Nous commands, "The squirrels must leave."

The white squirrel makes a 'who me' mime, while the black squirrel morphs into a big Black Squirrel Growling Monster.

Anza looks at him, "Good grief, not you too."

Nous points a Green Ray and the squirrels disappear. Nous continues, "You have seen where the problem started here on Theia. You must go to Earth, find the Sacred Oglala Crest and transport it back here along with the horse and the others."

Xandr looks concerned, "Is it too late for the White Calf Woman ceremony?"

"The ceremony has been rescheduled for another day."

Relieved, Xandr asks, "How do we find the Crest?"

"Gray Wolf took it when I was thrown from my horse." Anza looks unhappy.

"What do they want with it?" Payta inquires.

"They believe it will bring great wealth. They plan to sell it to the highest bidder; the one that promises the best opportunities for them."

"What about that awful Raven and Carl Drinkwater?" Xandr asks.

"The Raven wants to return here and be a Land Baron with riches, and more. Carl wants the same on Planet Earth."

"What is so special about the Crest"? Payta asks.

Nous has been listening to the kids and decides it's time to clear up the situation. "The primary function of the Sacred Crest is to unlock the secrets of the Tome of Legends and the Chronicle of Unchangeable Changes." Nous sees the bewildered look on the cousins faces. "It is not for you to understand. But, you can help Anza and Xandr."

"How?" asks Yellow Flower.

"We're just kids. How can we get it back from those bad guys on the other planet?" asks Little Bear.

Nous speaks softly, "Deception."

"Deception, but ---?" questions Little Flower.

"Deception and ... *MAGIC*."

Nous waves and the Stellar Bubble Craft appears in the sky swooping into the opening. It encompasses Nous and slowly moves through the forest creating a safe path surrounded by lavender leaves. The Stellar Bubble Craft rockets away when it reaches the outer edge of the Forest of Understanding.

Payta asks Anza, "What did that guy mean when he said deception and magic?"

"That's not just some guy. He's the balance keeper of our worlds," answers Xandr.

"Oh yeah. So, if he's the balancer, why doesn't he just wave his hand and get everything back in balance?"

"It's not that easy. We're gonna need your help with the deception so we can get it back."

"Yeah? What about the magic?"

"Leave that to me. You guys better get on home."

"How do we get outta here?"

"Follow the path that Nous created."

"But ---"

"No buts. We'll see you tomorrow."

The cousins run down the safe pathway as it closes in and disappears behind them.

With Bow and Cane in their hands, Anza and Xandr fly above the Forest to the Softwind farmhouse. They land and walk into the house.

"Where I'm gonna stay, is it near your Chamber Obscura?"

"Yes. It's down the hall and through the parlor."

Later that evening, they walk through the candlelit parlor where Moonshadow, Xandr's mother, is sewing a quilt and Lone Eagle, his father, is smoking a pipe and reading. Xandr stops at his mom and dad giving them childlike kisses on the cheek with a soft, "Goodnight, I love you." Anza waves goodnight and they continue to Xandr's room.

Xandr's parents sing out in unison, "Goodnight Anza."

The boys sit on Xandr's bed and discuss their plans.

"Tomorrow we go to Earth," Anza whispers, "but first we must read the Tome of Legends."

"We have to wait until mom and dad go to bed before we can go to my Chamber Obscura."

Chapter Twelve

The Chronicle of Unchangeable Changes

After a little while, Xandr sneaks out, and comes back with a big smile and a handful of cookies, "We can go now," handing Anza some cookies.

The boys are surprised to see Emera waiting in the Chamber Obscura. "Are you boys ready?"

Anza looks around, "This looks just like my Chamber Obscura except for the podium and the stuff on the walls."

Anza, Xandr and Emera stand at the podium, Anza on the left, Xandr on the right, Emera behind. Xandr points his left hand ring finger at the Chronicle of Unchangeable Changes. The pages glow and begin turning until the words and diagrams from the Tome of Legends appear.

Xandr asks, "Where do you want it to stop?"

Anza answers quickly, "We can only read some of it without the Sacred Oglala Crest or the Cosmic Eye Medallion. Let's see where it stops."

Emera instructs Xandr, "You must put your hand with the ring on the glowing page."

"Just me? Anza is the ---"

"Left hand on the page," Emera says with a stern look.

Xandr meekly places his left hand on the glowing page, which is on the Chronicle's right side. The left side page glows. Both sides of the Chronicle are glowing.

Emera nudges Anza, "Put your hand with the ring on the other page."

Anza looks at Xandr. Determined, he places his right hand on the left page. There is a small rumbling sound followed by some 'oh-oh what's happening music'.

A soft melodious voice comes from the Chronicle. "I am the Chronicle of Unchangeable Changes. I have many secrets. What do you wish to know?"

Anza and Xandr look at each other in disbelief.

"What are you? Is there someone in there? How can you talk?" asks Xandr.

"I am the Voice of Instruction."

Anza interjects, "We want to learn how to send the Sacred Oglala Crest and 'Runs like the Wind' and the Raven and some bad guys back here where they belong."

The Chronicle's glow intensifies, shimmers; it speaks, "To move the Sacred Oglala Crest trans-dimensionally you must energize its counterpart."

Anza asks, "What counterpart? Where is it?"

"It is the Cosmic Eye Medallion and is hidden in the podium in the Qi Chamber Obscura on Planet Earth."

"But it's all glass. There's no place to hide it."

"You must use your Magical Transfer Ring and ask the Podium to reveal the Cosmic Eye Medallion. Then summon me through the Tome of Legends. I will instruct you what to do next. Go with haste."

Anza and Xandr remove their hands from the book. The Chronicle's glow dissipates and the music stops.

Anza sings, "Hi ho, hi ho, it's off to Earth we go."

A mysterious force captures us and guides us to our seats in our spacecraft. Aboard Totfote and without any action from Solo or Duo we instantly find ourselves landing on Earth. Our Starcruiser dematerializes near the old barn. Our duplicates remain on Theia.

Chapter Thirteen

Masquerade

We return our sights to the Stellar Monitor and the Space-Between Dimensions.

Daiyu and Katipo are watching the Cosmos Comprehender. An image of Anza and Xandr in the Softwind Chamber Obscura is center screen.

Daiyu looks sternly at Katipo, "You must contact the Sheng Chi Master. Get him on your side. Convince him to help you get the Crest from Gray Wolf and Nigel so you can return it to Theia."

"He will be suspicious. He knows who I am."

"Take the form of Meilin. Make him believe it's to help the children, and of course, to save the world."

"He must know that the Raven must go with the horse and Crest as well as Gray Wolf and his band of Indians. What shall I promise him?"

"As Meilin ... you can't promise anything. You must plead with him for the best of, well, use your charm."

"You have not taught me the art of supplication."

Daiyu looks at Katipo with a master's glance while he points for her to leave.

Katipo bows and steps back. She stretches her arms out in front as she turns away, clicks her bracelets together forming radiant circles, and with a flash she zooms up and away towards Earth.

* * * * * * *

Solo manipulates the keypad as we set our sights on the Stellar Monitor and view the Residence of the Most High on the four-dimensional Planet of Anon.

Anon stands with his back to us watching the Cosmos Comprehender as the screen zooms in showing Katipo in flight. Two Grey Forms stand at his left.

"You must intercept Katipo."

The Grey Forms bow and dematerialize.

With a swift move of fingers on the Prompter keypad, Solo inputs the Earth view where we see the Sheng Chi Master sitting Buddha style in the meadow. The Grey Forms materialize looking like humans.

The Sheng Chi Master smiles, "I was wondering when you would arrive."

The Grey Forms stop abruptly putting their hands together as if in prayer, and bow to the Master intoning in unison, "Honorable Sheng Chi Master."

The Female Grey Form speaks, "We are here to intercept Katipo and keep her from getting the Sacred Oglala Crest from Gray Wolf and Nigel Churchill."

"Katipo? Hmm. What does she want with the Crest? Of course, of course, it is clear. Daiyu wants to use the power of the Sacred Crest to gain control on Theia."

The Male Grey Form responds. "Katipo will appear to you as Meilin, begging you to convince Gray Wolf and Nigel to give the Sacred Oglala Crest to her."

"To what avail?"

"She wants you to support her claim to shower them with riches."

"But, she does not have the power."

"Gray Wolf and Nigel do not know that."

"Gray Wolf thought I have magical powers to send them back to Theia. I misled him to believe I could not, and that he needs to find another way. He will certainly seek out Tian yì to do that."

"Tian yì has just learned of his power to send the Crest and 'Runs like the Wind' back to Theia. But, he wants to keep the horse for himself on Earth."

"Does he know the horse and raven must be returned with the Sacred Crest?"

* * * * * * *

Katipo lands in the meadow not far from where the Grey Forms landed. She looks around and sees the Sheng Chi Master and the Grey Forms in the distance. She morphs into Meilin Bancroft-Qi wearing her earth costume; blue jeans, a jacket over her blouse, a cowboy hat and boots and walks to the road a few moments after the Grey Forms leave the Sheng Chi Master.

The Grey Forms, dressed as evangelical humans, walk in the center of the road with bibles and purposely block Ka-tipo-Meilin as they come upon her. Katipo-Meilin courteously steps aside to allow the Grey Forms to pass, but they sidestep causing her to stop.

The Male Grey Form raises his hand holding a bible. "You should not continue. There is danger that way."

"What danger? I see nothing but an empty road."

"You are Meilin, mother of the boy Anza. We have come from beyond, down the road," he points, "there are people that want to steal what you have, and will hurt you to get it."

The Female Grey Form intercedes, "Come sister, we will walk with you. You will be safe with us."

"Safe? But I ---"

"Not to worry."

"How do you know of Anza, and what do these dangerous people want of me?"

"They know of his ... abilities. Come."

The Grey Forms position themselves on each side, holding her arms, and escort the reluctant Katipo-Meilin to the Qi farmhouse.

Katipo-Meilin struggles and finally pulls away from the Grey Forms as they reach the Qi farmhouse.

"Go away, leave me. I am home. I will be safe."

Phir hears the ruckus and looks out the window. He sees Katipo-Meilin and the Grey Forms. He looks back to see Meilin sitting at the table. A surprised look comes over his face as he looks back out the window.

The Grey Forms attempt to stop Katipo-Meilin as she struggles away. She finally frees herself from their restraint and reaches under her jacket. She clicks on her belt buckle, raises her hands above her head and pulls the imaginary converter down the length of her body, and morphs back into Katipo wearing her Latrodectus outfit.

Phir asks himself, 'Where is Anza?'

Katipo stretches her arms out in front and clicks her bracelets together. An energy field broadcasts radiant circles as she raises her arms and zooms up and away. The Grey Forms look at each other with dismay.

Chapter Fourteen

Cosmic Eye Medallion

Anza and Xandr are standing at the podium in the Chamber Obscura on Earth. Anza points his Ring at the Podium and nothing happens.

Xandr questions Anza, "Aren't you 'sposed to ask it to show us the medallion?"

"Oh yeah," he points at the podium, "show the medallion," he looks at Xandr bewildered. "It isn't doing anything."

"Cosmic Eye. You gotta tell it to show the cosmic eye medallion."

"The words were different. It wasn't show," he thinks, "it was," he puts his hands on the sides of his head and shakes his head as if to rattle the answer loose from his brain, "reveal, that's it." He points his ring finger again. "Reveal the Cosmic Eye Medallion."

The Podium starts shaking for a few moments and stops as quickly as it started. A blue light shines from a point in the podium immediately below the glass top. Anza sees the Cosmic Eye Medallion glowing inside the Podium supporting shaft.

"Ok. So now what?" Anza asks.

"We gotta ask the book to ---"

"Ri-i-ight. I s'pose we gotta do the hands-on-the-book-thing again."

Anza positions himself on the left side and Xandr stands on the right. Anza starts the ritual by pointing his Ring finger at the Tome of Legends. The pages turn and suddenly stop leaving the left side page aglow. Anza carefully places his Ring finger on the left glowing page and the right side page begins to glow.

"Your turn."

Xandr slowly places his ring finger on the glowing page on the right side of the Tome. The familiar rumbling sound followed by the 'oh-oh what's happening music' begins.

A soft melodious voice coming from the large white book interrupts the music. "I am the Tome of Legends. I have many secrets. What do you wish to know?"

Anza and Xandr look at each other in awe.

Anza talks to the Tome of Legends, "You sound just like the Chronicle of Unchangeable Changes."

"We are the same, but different. Do you wish to speak with the Chronicle?"

"Yes. We want to use the Cosmic Eye Medallion to find the Sacred Oglala Crest."

"We will instruct you. You will be speaking to the Chronicle of Unchangeable Changes in the other world. You must speak to it in your native language."

Anza speaks to the Chronicle of Unchangeable Changes in Chinese, 'How do I use the Cosmic Eye Medallion?' "Wo rúhé shiyòng yuzhòu zhi yan jiangzhang?"

The Chronicle of Unchangeable Changes responds through the Tome of Legends in English, "Point your Transfer Ring at the podium, and command it to release the Cosmic Eye Medallion."

A blue laser-like light shines making the podium vibrate as Anza points his ring finger at the podium, "shìfàng de yuzhòu zhi yan jiangzhang."

The Cosmic Eye Medallion, a concave variegated blue translucent enneagon crystal with an eye in the middle appears and slowly sails out of the podium into Anza's hand. He instinctively sets his thumb in an indentation at the bottom.

The Eye of the Medallion glows brighter and brighter until a laser-type blue light snaps out projecting a holographic image of Gray Wolf holding the Crest.

Anza is calm.

"Wow!" shouts Xandr.

Gray Wolf looks up.

"That's Gray Wolf. D'you think maybe he heard me?"

"Maybe. Let's check it out."

Xandr whispers, "So-o-o what if he can?"

Anza shrugs his shoulders and looks back at the hologram calling out in a lowered, rough sounding voice, "I want my Crest!"

Gray Wolf, in the hologram, looks bewildered, "Who said that?"

Anza and Xandr snicker as thirteen-year-old boys do.

"You must return the Crest or face the consequences," Anza commands in his animated voice.

Gray Wolf, in the hologram, looks around. The image shimmers with static.

"Where are you? Show yourself, or I'll ---"

"You'll do nothing. Put the Crest down and leave."

Anza tightens his thumb on the Medallion. There is a sharp cracking sound in the hologram. Gray Wolf looks around and cowers.

"How'd you do that?" Xandr whispers.

"Don't know. I didn't do anything special, just wished it and the Medallion ... I dunno ... so-o-o maybe it ---"

Xandr, still looking at the hologram, shouts, "Look out ... the raven."

Gray Wolf ducks as the Raven files into the hologram and swoops down, snatches the Crest from his hand, squawks, and flies away. Anza tightens his thumb on the Medallion. There is a loud cracking sound and the hologram sputters and fades away.

Xandr is confused, "What happened?"

"I don't have a clue."

Anza points his ring finger at the Tome of Legends. The pages glow as the Tome questions, "How can I help you?"

"The Crest was stolen again. How do I find it?"

"Do you wish to speak with the Chronicle of Unchangeable Changes?"

* * * * * * *

Airborne Katipo spots the Raven taking the Crest from Gray Wolf. She takes chase and rapidly catches up with the unsuspecting Bird. She clicks her bracelets together causing an energy field to broadcast radiant circles, which engulfs the Raven. Overpowered he struggles, but cannot maintain flight and falls.

Katipo lands and catches the stunned Raven removing the Crest from its talons and puts the bird on the ground, "Now that I have the Crest. I rule!"

"There is more to it than just having the Crest."

"More? What?"

"The Crest is only powerful if you know how to read the inscriptions."

"What Inscriptions"?

"Look," he points at the Crest, "on the edges. There are ancient inscriptions that can only be deciphered with the Cosmic Eye Medallion that Anza has, together with the corresponding codes in the Tome of Legends."

"My Magical Transfer Ring will allow me to read the secrets of the Tome of Legends."

"It will give you access, but no secrets."

Katipo touches the Abstract Data Recorder on her Belt Buckle, looks down at the Raven with a sinister smile. "Do you know how to read the inscriptions?"

"I know the secret. You need me." He lies.

"What makes you think I need you?"

"You need what I know," the nervous bird compounds his falsehood, "there's more. You must have the Cosmic Eye Medallion on Earth. The real power is to have both the Crest and the Medallion."

"You think I need both?"

"The Tome of Legends here and the Chronicle of Unchangeable Changes on Theia work together as one."

"Where do I find the Medallion?"

"The Chosen One has it."

Katipo swirls her Cloak about herself and disappears.

* * * * * * *

Anza and Xandr sit on the straw covered floor inside a Circle of Stones.

Anza looks down at the stones, "I gotta get away from all this stuff."

"But you've gotta find the Crest and get it back with the saddle and my horse and ---"

"I'm going for a ride."

Anza jumps up, walks to the Bronze Statue. The statue stands rigid. Suddenly its eyes open.

Anza closes his eyes and points his ring finger at the horse, "Lái shenghuó ... lái shenghuó."

The Bronze Statue sheds its metal coat and comes alive. The horse extends his foreleg scratching the barn floor and walks to Anza. Anza climbs on a hay bale, mounts the horse and rides out.

Anza races the horse down the dirt road. Suddenly a swirl of dust appears a short distance away. Anza reins in. The swirl becomes Katipo's cloak slowly revealing Katipo. "Hello Anza."

Katipo points her right hand ring finger at Anza lifting him from his horse guiding him slowly to the ground.

"How do you know my name? Who are you?"

"I am called Katipo. I am from the Space-Between Dimensions."

"Space between? What do you want with me?"

"Something is missing from your horse's saddle," she points, "there, on the side. See?"

Anza does not look. Katipo puts her hand beneath her belt buckle drawing it back out. She slowly opens her hand with the Crest. Anza looks at the Crest without emotion.

"It looks like an old piece of junk. The saddle doesn't need that, besides ---"

"Don't play innocent with me. I know where that horse is from, and where it belongs. It --"

"He's my horse, and he belongs here with me."

"February 29th will soon be here, and you must send him and the saddle back to the other world. Oh, and don't forget that despicable raven. He must go too."

"Why are you telling me this?"

"I'll trade the Crest for your Medallion."

"Medallion? I've gotta go."

"Let me know when you want the Crest. Tell the Grey Forms ... they'll know how to find me."

"I gotta go."

Katipo points her ring finger at Anza. Lifting him slowly and gently positioning him on the saddle.

"Later!" Katipo swirls the cloak around herself and disappears.

The horse rears, Anza jams both heels into his sides and they gallop away.

* * * * * * *

Anza is lying on his bed and hears the 'start-the-race' trumpet sound. He sits up and sees the Oracle Frame glowing. He puts his ring on and taps the screen.

Xandr appears, "Hi Anza."

"Hi. Are you back home?"

"Yes. Nous showed me how to travel here by myself. One minute I was there, and then I am home. Did you find the Crest?"

"I met this person from the Space-Between Dimensions; she has the Crest, and wants to trade it for the Medallion."

"She has the Crest? But, we saw the raven get it. Whose side is she on?"

"I'm not sure. She didn't seem like a bad guy. Ya know, I think she's the same one that pretended to be my mother a few days ago. Besides, she has a ring like ours, and can do magic stuff."

"Magic? What kind of magic stuff?"

"She pointed her ring and lifted me off my horse, and later put me back."

"Can we do that kind of magic?"

"I don't know; haven't tried yet."

"So, how does she know about the Medallion and why does she want the Crest?"

"I don't know, but time is running out. And, and ... I'm so-o-o confused; the raven ... Nigel ... Gray Wolf ... now this person from wherever. I gotta talk to Yeye. Later!"

Anza turns the Oracle off. With a baffled look he raises his head, "Why me?" Expecting an answer and not getting one he pulls the covers back and slides under. He tosses and turns with visions of the Earth exploding like his previous dream. Finally, he goes into a deep and different kind of sleep traveling outside of his body into the depths of outer space.

Solo is studying the Stellar Monitor, looks over to Duo and says, "Something is happening to Anza in his sleep. He is trans-dimensionally traveling without knowing. This could be dangerous for him."

"We need to track him and see where he goes."

Duo works his magic bringing Anza's sleep travel up on the Stellar Monitor where we see him tumbling and tossing as he rockets through meteorite infested deep space on what seems like an endless trip past the four-dimensional world to the Space-Between Dimensions.

"Yeow!" he screams as he barely escapes a huge meteor on an apparent collision course with him. Suddenly aware of the danger, he readies his flight to avoid the oncoming projectiles.

His trans-dimensional travel slows to a mere mach one jet speed as the incredible journey comes to a sudden end. The bewildered Anza lands with a thud on a firm cloud-like floor. He shakes off his fear and gets up to find himself standing ten feet in front of the Black Jade with Katipo at his side.

The space is as nondescript as any semi-transparent enclosure could be with the blackness of outer space encircling everything.

"What is this place?"

"You surely remember me," Katipo interjects.

The thirteen year old boy inspects Katipo, but his eyes soon become transfixed on the awesome figure of the Black Jade, "You," he directs his question, "who and what are you?"

The Black Jade spreads his wings to show his power, and quickly aims at a point near to where Anza is standing releasing a mild lightning bolt to frighten him, "I am Daiyu, the ruler of the planets." He snaps another bolt stopping it short of Anza's midsection. With a move of his hand, he raises him up and guides him closer as he sits on his colossal throne of gilded wood.

Anza struggles with the overpowering invisible restraints. "Let me go."

Daiyu wiggles his index finger lowering his captive with a thud.

"Thanks for nothing; you overgrown parasite."

The Black Jade glances at Katipo, "The Chosen One has a lot of spunk."

Katipo nods in agreement.

Daiyu roars with an obnoxiously loud laugh as he looks down on Anza. "Overgrown," he pauses, "not big enough, but powerful enough to suck the blood from your earthly form."

Katipo is shocked to hear the abusive discourse and whispers, "You must not hurt him."

Daiyu, not accustomed to confrontation from his protégé, growls, "What would you have me do?"

Daiyu gestures sending a magnetic sound barrier in front of Anza, "This will keep him from hearing us."

"He must be convinced to help with the cipher." Katipo suggests.

"I will put a spell on him that will control his actions."

"The Chosen One is endowed with great magic that must also be thwarted. Will your spell keep him from using his magic against you?"

"I am more powerful than he is."

"What is next?"

"I will send him back to Earth in a sleep mode. When he wakens, he will remember his trip to the Space-Between Dimensions as a pleasant encounter, and I will control him."

Daiyu motions removing the sound barrier and sends another lightning bolt at Anza creating an energy field around him sending him off to Earth through the meteorite showers.

Anza snaps out of the sleep mode becoming aware of the situation as he speeds uncontrollably toward home. He calls to Nous for help.

Solo and Duo have the Stellar Monitor focused on Anza in deep space and we see Nous approaching.

The Stellar Bubble Craft zooms through outer space pulling up next to Anza as he is entering the atmosphere. The Craft opens and draws him in carefully. He falls back into a sleep mode as Nous transports him back to the safety of his bed.

Duo positions the Stellar Monitor back to the happenings on Earth.

The next morning Anza is awaken by his grandfather. "Wake up sleepy head. You have much to do."

After breakfast, Anza and his grandfather go for a walk to the Path of Knowledge and sit under the Sugi tree.

Anza tells Phir Qi of his nighttime dream travel to the Space-Between Dimensions finishing with, "But, it felt real, and there was more happening. It wasn't just all those meteorites and four-dimensional images."

"How do you know it was the Space-Between Dimensions? Did you meet someone there?"

"I think so, Katipo maybe, but it's kinda fuzzy."

"I'll work some of my own magic and we'll find out what you saw, but we'll ... you will have to go through the Dream Recovery Protocol."

The black Raccoon appears in front of them.

Phir calls out, "What do you want?"

Notso replies, "I want to help."

"Help? How?"

"I've been watching the raven ... the bad guys from the other planet ... Gray Wolf ... all of ---"

"Get on with it."

Notso looks at Anza, "You have the Cosmic Eye Medallion."

Phir looks at Anza, "You have? Of course you do."

"We can watch what they are doing." says Notso with confidence. Phir skeptically looks at him.

Phir turns back to Anza. "You know how to ---?"

"Yes."

Anza takes the Medallion from his pocket and sets his thumb firmly in an indentation at the bottom. The eye of the medallion glows, brighter, brighter, and then a laser type blue light projects a three-dimensional holographic image of Gray Wolf.

Surprised, he drops the Medallion, and looks to Phir who motions for him to pick it up.

Anza cautiously picks it up and presses his thumb repeatedly, pointing, until there are more images; Gray Wolf is still sitting on the ground as the Sheng Chi Master enters the hologram. They fadeout and are replaced with an image of the raven in the cave talking with an image of Dimitri in the pool.

"Whoa," sings Notso as an image of Katipo appears inspecting the Crest.

The images fade, "Yeye? What can I do? They all want the Crest for different reasons."

Notso walks slowly to Anza, "I can get the Crest from Katipo when she sleeps."

"That's too risky. I'll find a way."

Phir looks at Anza, "We must go to the Chamber Obscura and use the Tome to access the Chronicle of Unchangeable Changes. It will tell us what to do, not this raccoon"

Notso tries to defend his presence and brings more doubt to the situation. "Where is this Chronicle, and why is it called Unchangeable Changes? How can there be changes that you can't change?"

Anza dismisses the raccoon, "You don't know anything," he calls out, "Nous ... Nous."

The Bubble Craft moves toward Anza and slowly lowers to a point two feet above the ground. The Craft flies off as Nous hovers.

Nous speaks in a childlike voice, "Ahh, you wish for assistance to enlighten the critter. Or perhaps there is another reason you summon me."

"It's not about him. I want to know the mystery of the unchangeable changes."

"Change is the only thing that is constant," Nous pauses, "even when we struggle to maintain the dynamic balance of the opposite planets." Nous looks at Anza and Notso. "If one planet changes ... the other must also change, or they both will be destroyed."

"That's why the crest and raven must go back to Planet Theia. Right?"

"And, the others must also go back."

Nous moves closer. "The Unchangeable is the Ultimate Presence. The Ultimate Presence will not change with the flow of time as *you* know it ... the evolution of events change to the unchangeable, and is no more. When you Paesre you become one with the embodiment of Ultimate Duration."

Phir looks at his grandson, "Do you understand, Sūnzi?"

"Sort of Yeye," he shrugs his shoulders, "not really." he turns to Nous, "What am I 'sposed to do now?"

"Go with your grandfather to the place where you learn from the Chronicle of Unchangeable Changes. There you will discover more about the Unchangeable. You must use the Sacred Oglala Bow in addition to your Transfer Ring and the Cosmic Eye Medallion to gain access to the Trans-dimensional formula that is necessary to send these objects to their rightful place."

"What about the Crest?"

"Go now and learn."

Nous waves and the Stellar Bubble Craft appears in the distant sky and swoops in as before, encompassing Nous as it flies away.

Anza and Phir turn and walk away.

"What about me?" Notso calls out.

Anza waves goodbye without a sound.

Chapter Fifteen
The Sheng Chi Master

The Sheng Chi Master is sitting Buddha style under the Earthly Cedar Tree mediating. Gray Wolf approaches on the dirt road with a battle spear in his hand. He sits down quietly next to the Sheng Chi Master with the spear resting easy across his legs. He waits.

After a while the Sheng Chi Master, his eyes closed and still in his meditative posture, breaks the silence. "You have not found a way to return to your home. You come for guidance?"

"You lied to me."

"No lie. It is the way of the Thunder Beings, they ---"

A flash of lightning interrupts the Master. Gray Wolf looks toward the sky. The Sheng Chi Master remains calm, while Gray Wolf stands up.

"What's that?" Gray Wolf points to a cloudless sky.

The Stellar Bubble Craft appears; zooms down toward them at lightning speed, stops abruptly hovering two feet above the dirt road. Nous does not move out and hover as usual, but steps out standing with feet an inch off the ground. The Craft flies off.

The Sheng Chi Master looks up. "It is good to see you again.

"It has been too long, Sheng Chi Master," Nous looks at Gray Wolf and back to the Master, "Gray Wolf wants you to send him back to Theia with the Sacred Oglala Crest. But he ---"

"Who are you, and what do you want?" asks Grey Wolf.

"I am Nous; the Equilibrium. I am the keeper of planetary balance. You do not belong here and you must return to your planet or ---"

He interrupts again. "Equilibrium? Ha! Return? Not until I get what I came for." He points at the Sheng Chi Master, "He has tricked me." Gray Wolf raises his voice and turns to Nous, "You are in the way. Go. Leave us."

Nous looks at the Sheng Chi Master, turns to inspect Gray Wolf, considers the situation, and moves slightly extending a hand toward Gray Wolf. A green ray discharges slowly from the index finger pointing directly at Gray Wolf's chest with a slight 'thud'; a moment passes and Gray Wolf wavers dropping to his knees stunned.

Nous looks at the Sheng Chi Master, "Leave us old friend, we have a difference to settle."

The Sheng Chi Master gets up, bows reverently, turns and departs. Gray Wolf gets up and shakes off the stun as he brandishes his spear. He lunges toward Nous with a battle cry, "Hoka Hey!"

Nous parries. The fight is on as Gray Wolf positions his Buffalo Horn War Spear toward Nous. There is a 'flash' from the spear point. Nous ducks warding off the spear burst with his Green Ray. There are many volleys. The flashes from both back and forth seem unending until Nous' Green Ray snaps Gray Wolf's spear in two. Gray Wolf looks bewildered and retreats.

The Bubble Craft retrieves Nous and speeds away.

"You haven't won," Gray Wolf shouts, 'beware' in Lakota, "Iwakta ye." He reaches down to the dirt road, grabs a handful of dust. The throws it up in the air as unearthly indistinguishable ghostly images appear then disappear in the dust. He turns away mounting his horse and rides off shouting beware the Ghost Dancers in Lakota, "Iwakta ye Howiwacipi."

A few miles down the road, Gray Wolf meets up with his group of scoundrels and gallops off to meet Nigel.

Nicholas Gray Wolf and his cohorts rein in their mounts just short of Nigel Churchill, who is standing by his horse on the side of the road.

"The one that calls himself the Equilibrium has great powers and says we must return to the Planet Theia with the horse and Crest," bellows Gray Wolf.

"When do you plan to return?" asks Nigel.

"Not before we get the treasures. Drinkwater will be a problem because he lives here and doesn't care if the Crest and horse stay here, and that black bird; he's crazy enough to mess everything up with his greed." Gray Wolf says with authority.

Nigel looks at the band of Indians, "Where are Drinkwater and the bird?"

"Dunno about Drinkwater, but the bird always goes to the same cave."

"Let's go."

Chapter Sixteen

Raccoons and Owl

Back at the cave, the Raven is sitting on a rock by the pool looking into the water. Slowly a reflection appears changing into a vision of Dimitri Talbot.

The reflection speaks as Carl Drinkwater enters. "We must get the Crest back from Katipo."

"She sometimes pretends to be Missus Qi. I've seen her snooping around in the barn and changing into that ... that ... Spider Person."

"Spider? You saw her change to a spider?"

"Well, not a real spider. She has a spider pitcher on her," he points to his chest, "ya know? And she's pretty ... like a ... a ... angel sort of ... the way she flies off."

"Do you know where she is now?"

"She sometimes sits under the safe tree."

The reflection of Dimitri dissipates and the Raven flies out of the cave. He sees Nigel and Gray Wolf and their band of outlaws in the distance. Knowing they will do anything to get the crest, he morphs into a Great Horned Owl and flies to the Sacred Chinese Cedar Tree to spy on them without being suspected.

Katipo, wearing her Latrodectus outfit is sitting under the Sugi Tree in meditation. Her Chota Invisibility Cloak is covering her legs and one shoulder.

There are spies watching; Dimitri, as the Owl, perches on a branch patiently waiting for a chance to swoop down and grab the Crest, and the Black Raccoon is lingering in the shadows of the tree as Carl Drinkwater searches the road with a flashlight in his hand. Carl stops waving his hand as the flashlight beam catches Katipo. He jumps back in surprise.

Katipo opens her eyes. "Hello Carl. Come ... come sit with me ... here by my side," she pats the ground.

"Where's the rest of you?"

"Oh ... here, let me move my cloak."

Katipo moves her cloak down and away, exposing her legs, but still hiding her shoulder. Carl stares in awe.

"It's just my cloak. Do not be afraid. It makes me invisible whenever I want," she moves the cloak again, this time revealing the rest of her in the black form-fitting Latrodectus attire. She swirls the cloak placing it on the ground next to her in an invisible condition.

He looks at her and smiles as he sits near.

The mesmerized Carl asks, "What can I do for you?"

Katipo knows she has gained an ally, and asks his help to gain access to the Secret Room.

* * * * * * *

Anza and Phir are in the Chamber Obscura standing at the podium. The Sacred Oglala Bow rests against the podium.

Phir is instructing Anza, "When you were with Xandr you were able to move trans-dimensionally because you used both Transfer Rings together," Phir pauses to be sure his grandson understands, "when you are alone you need the

Sacred Oglala Bow and the Cosmic Eye Medallion with your ring."

"How did I travel to the Space-Between Dimensions without any of those things?"

"We'll get to that later when I take you through the Dream Recovery Protocol." Phir hands Anza the Bow, "Think the command, and use the Bow and Cosmic Eye Medallion with your ring to travel. Do not linger in space; come right back. We have much to do."

Anza points his ring finger and raises the Bow in his left hand while holding the Medallion in his right hand. He rises slowly. Then with a rocket-like surge, he flies up and through the star-like ceiling into outer space beyond Earth, past an image of the four-dimensional world, around the Sun to a view of Planet Theia. He pauses for a brief moment and turns back retracing his path to Earth.

Anza flies through the star-like ceiling, landing next to Phir in the Chamber Obscura. "Wow! That was fun."

"Sūnzi!"

"Ok ... Ok."

"Let's take a walk."

*　*　*　*　*　*　*

Katipo is walking along the dirt road examining the Crest. The Great Horned Owl flies high above watching her every move with a readiness to attack. Suddenly the Black Raccoon appears in front of her.

"What do you want, Raccoon?"

"I want the Crest."

"Why should I give it to you? What would a little raccoon do with this Crest?"

Obviously insulted, the Raccoon says, "Little? Little?"

"Oh. Go away and don't bother me."

Katipo walks away from the raccoon, but he jumps at her grabbing for the Crest. Katipo dodges.

"Gimme that crest or I'll ---"

"You'll do nothing you obnoxious little creature."

Notso positions itself like a bull ready for the charge, pawing the ground. He morphs into a huge ten-foot-tall Gnashing Teeth Black Raccoon Monster. "Not so little ... little girl. Give me the crest or ---"

Katipo interrupts the Notso giant, "Or what, you pathetic critter?"

The circling Great Horned Owl sees an opportunity to get the Crest, sets its wings to the full sixty-inch span, and stealthy dive bombs Katipo at the exact moment as the Raccoon Hulk lurches at Katipo.

Katipo is unaware of the silent Owl, but whirls her Cloak around herself to avoid the Raccoon Hulk. She sidesteps and disappears under the cloak.

The Owl smashes into the Hulk Raccoon and falls to the ground dazed.

The Hulk Raccoon searches around and gets angrier and angrier taking a swipe at the Owl.

The Owl spreads its massive wings and with incredible ease instantly soars away gaining an advantageous viewpoint from high above. Undetected, he watches Katipo's stealth movement as the landscape disappears and reappears under her cloak revealing her path toward the Qi Farm.

The bewildered Hulk Raccoon returns to normal size and scampers down the road toward the old barn.

Katipo comes to the Qi farm and takes refuge in a corner horse stall of the old barn. She looks around and closes the stall door placing her cloak on the hay-covered floor. Unbeknownst to her, the White Raccoon watches from behind a hay bale. Katipo lies on the cloak while hiding the Crest under the cloak. The exhausted Katipo falls into a deep sleep. The White Raccoon waits until he hears her heavy breathing, and slowly creeps under the stall door toward Katipo. Carefully removing the Crest, he quietly runs away with the cipher in his mouth and peeks into the Grand Room window. The Great Horned Owl (Raven) is watching from the rooftop.

Anza, with the Oglala Bow in hand, and his grandfather return and are walking to the Chamber Obscura through the Grand Room when Anza notices the white raccoon watching from the window with the crest in its mouth.

"Look Yeye. The white raccoon has the Crest."

"So it does, so it does," he motions to the raccoon. "Go to the kitchen door and bring it here. Quietly, so your Mom and Dad won't hear you. Take the Bow."

The massive Owl swoops down, grabs the unsuspecting white raccoon in its talons and begins to fly off as Anza runs out. He raises the Bow intuitively stopping the Owl's flight; he enlists the magic of the deer's tail and carefully lowers the massive bird. The Owl is powerless as he removes the raccoon and Crest from its grasp. With a quick motion, he releases the Owl and watches it fly off as he goes into the house.

Anza moves quickly through the kitchen to the Great Room with the White Raccoon in his arms.

"The Owl tried---"

"I know."

"How ---?"

"Cover its eyes."

Phir makes his normal arm gestures and incantation, soon the wall opens. They go into the Chamber Obscura.

"Put the critter on the chair."

The Raccoon takes the crest from its mouth, looks around and opens its mouth to speak.

"Not a sound or I'll send you to outer space forever," Phir Qi says with the authority of a drill sergeant.

The Raccoon attempts to hide the Crest with its paw, but is not fast enough for the observant Phir Qi.

Phir stretches his arm out commanding the raccoon, "The Crest."

The Raccoon takes the Crest and begins to speak.

Phir moves his hand toward the Raccoon. "Silence, give me the Crest."

The raccoon unwillingly gives the Crest to Phir.

"It's time for your lesson."

"The raccoon ... it'll hear."

"Use the Bow."

Anza smiles, raising the Bow and speaks 'you cannot hear' in Chinese, "In ting bù dào."

"You must understand more about the unchangeable, before we continue your lessons in the magic of trans-travel, especially how you traveled to the Space-Between Dimensions without your ring and bow. We will start with the Dream Recovery Protocol."

"Did I do something wrong?"

"No. Be at peace; you must Paesre."

Anza becomes calm as Phir raises the Bow and draws imaginary circles around him transposing him into a holographic image traveling through space toward the Space-Between Dimensions while he stays safely in the Chamber of Obscura.

The Tome of Legends begins to glow as the hologram acquires data from the transference and sends the information to the Chronicle of Unchangeable Changes.

The Chronicle speaks through the Tome, "I am engaging the Dream Recovery Protocol."

The hologram fluctuates as the image changes into two images of Anza. One image speeds away to outer space as the other remains in an apparent sleep mode.

The Chronicle continues, "The Chosen One has acquired the nature of Paesre and traveled in the dream state to a dangerous place in deep space without the assistance of his Sacred Oglala Bow or Magical Transfer Ring. This method of transportation is much too advanced for the novice Chosen One and should be curtailed until he is more experienced. He is fortunate to have survived his encounter with the Black Jade."

Phir lowers the Bow; the hologram sputters and fades away as Anza returns to an awakened state.

"What happened? I was able to see and hear everything from the Chronicle while I was in the hologram."

"That is the nature of the Dream Recovery Protocol."

"How do I keep from doing that again?"

"Control; you need to be aware and practice control."

Chapter Seventeen

The Other Horse

Anza is riding 'Runs like the Wind' in the meadow as Qingling races up riding bareback. They join up and stop to talk.

"Where'd ya get the horse?" Anza asks, "He's beautiful."

"I found him on your farm way over there," she points.

"Who does he belong to?"

"You, I s'pose ... I mean ... he's on your farm ... maybe he could be from ... na-a-h ---"

"What should we call him?"

"How about calling him Lightning?"

"Why?"

"Well, it was raining and lightning and thundering when I found him. I went under the old lean-to so's I wouldn't get wet, and there he was.

"Lightning and Thundering. Thunder, I like Thunder."

"Me too; me too! Let's go!"

Anza and Qingling race toward a distant meadow.

Gray Wolf and the four bad guys spot the kids, and give chase. Anza and Qingling see them and urge their horses into a gallop, but it is too late. The bad guys cut them off on a diagonal path.

"Hold up." Gray Wolf motions to the kids with a rifle in hand.

"What do you want?" Anza shouts.

"We'll talk about that later. Get their reins. Take them to the cave."

The kids try to get away, but are surrounded. They unwillingly succumb to the capture.

One of the bad guys reaches over and grabs the reins of Anza's horse while another guy throws a lasso over Qingling's horse. They ride down the path with Gray Wolf and the other bad guys taking up the rear.

The short ride seems like a horrifically long journey as the bad guys lead Anza and Qingling to the Cave entrance. Gray Wolf motions for them to dismount. The bad guy pulls the reins over 'Runs like the Wind's nose causing him to rear, which spooks Thunder. Thunder reacts and rears with his forelegs thrashing aggressively. Without reins, Qingling grabs the mane, but is unable to control her mount and attempts an emergency dismount. Thunder moves violently throwing his bareback rider to the ground. Qingling receives a hard blow to her head rendering her unconscious. Thunder raises his head, snorts and bolts away.

Anza dismounts and rushes to Qingling. Traumatized by the happening he starts wailing.

"Shut up kid." Gray Wolf hollers as he prods Qingling with his foot. Anza tries to wake her up, but his cousin does not move.

Gray Wolf pulls Anza away from Qingling passing him off to one of the bad guys. "Take him into the cave."

"Leave me alone," Anza Kungfu kicks the bad guy, "she's hurt. I gotta help her."

Another bad guy grabs Anza and drags him into the cave. He struggles and resists with Shaolin Kungfu moves, but the bad guy is too big and smacks him hard. Anza falls to the ground and crawls away into the darkness of the cave opening.

"Tie the horse to that tree."

"What about the other kid?"

"Leave her."

* * * * * * *

We return our sights to the Stellar Monitor and the Residence of the Most High where Anon is watching the Cosmos Comprehender in dismay with two Grey Forms standing at his left side. With a sigh and a sad voice, he utters a solemn command. "Summon Nous."

* * * * * * *

Duo prompts the Stellar Monitor back to Earth as Thunder races down the road toward the Qi Farm coming to a stop near the old barn. A farmhand lassoes him and leads the unwilling horse toward the corral.

Phir is looking out the kitchen window at the riderless horse with a worried look as he talks on his mobile phone. He walks out of the house and motions for the farmhand to stop as he inspects the horse. Intuitively he knows the horse is the counterpart to 'Runs like the Wind'. "I'll call you back," he tells the mobile phone.

Phir is concerned about Anza, and runs into the old barn. The Owl atop the house eave has been watching Thunder's arrival, morphs into the Raven, flies in after Phir and perches up in the rafters. The Black Raccoon is watching the activity from behind a hay bale.

Phir looks around and sees Carl Drinkwater.

"Good morning Carl."

"Good morning sir."

"Have you seen my grandson?"

"No sir."

"The horse, where's the statue?

"Don't know. Didn't even notice it was missing. Who do you suppose it might of ---?"

"Bring my car around ... no ... the pick-up, and my rifle and a box of ammo. Be sure it's loaded."

"Yes sir."

Carl leaves the barn while Phir stays to inspect. He sees the raven and raccoon, but doesn't acknowledge their presence. He hears a rustling in one of the stalls, and notices the semi invisible nature of the straw in the floor. He knows Katipo is hiding under her cloak and leaves with satisfaction.

Carl brings the pick-up around, "Your rifle's loaded; the extra shells are on the seat."

"Call me when you see my grandson."

"Yes sir."

Katipo awakens to the ruckus and realizes the Crest is gone from under her Cloak.

The Black Raccoon sneaks out and jumps into the back of the pick-up unnoticed while the Raven flies out to track the pick-up. Katipo disappears under the cover of her cloak.

Phir drives his pick-up on the dirt road. He stops and pulls off the road. The Black Raccoon jumps out of the truck bed. The Raven flies to a tree branch for a good viewing spot, morphing once again into an Owl. Phir gets out of truck with binoculars in hand; he scans the terrain stopping his search near the base of the mountainside and sees a horse outside a cave entrance. He recognizes it as 'Runs like the Wind'.

Phir sets the binoculars down grabs his rifle in one hand, raises the Oglala Bow with the other hand and flies to the horse's side. He checks Qingling and gets a concerned look on his face. He lifts the Bow to the sky in a ceremonial fashion.

"Nous. I need your help."

A moment later, the Stellar Bubble Craft appears in the distant sky rocketing directly to Phir and Qingling.

The Craft hovers, lowers to rest two feet above the ground next to Phir. Nous looks around, considers the situation and goes to Qingling with an extended hand. The light milieu surrounding Nous brightens as it expands to encompass Qingling. A Green Ray shoots from Nous' finger shinning directly on Qingling's forehead. After a brief moment, Qingling stirs and awakens, but is a little groggy.

The light shroud diminishes as Nous extends a hand, "Come child." Turning to Phir with a convincing glance, "I'll take her home. Set the horse free and leave."

"What about my grandson?

"I'll be back for him. Do not worry."

Qingling walks slowly and unsteady toward Nous. With a slight motion, Nous summons the ethereal light from the waiting Craft. It surrounds Nous and Qingling drawing them in. They disappear inside the Craft as it rockets away.

Phir unties the horse swatting its rump with his rifle barrel. The horse runs back to the farm with Phir in his pickup a short distance behind.

Chapter Eighteen
Katipo's Revelation

Katipo, still under her cloak in the horse stall watches a holographic image of Phir, Qingling and Nous. She waves her hand and the holograph disappears. She removes the cloak and walks out of the stall to the doorway; looks around and stretches her arms out in front, clicks her bracelets together forming radiant circles and flies out the door to a place near the cave as Nous is returning for Anza.

Nous nods to acknowledge her arrival.

Katipo, with hands together as if in prayer bows and says, "The children are not supposed to be hurt."

"I am gratified to hear you speak with concern for the children."

"Daiyu sent me to get the Crest."

"Yes, I know. The Black Jade wants the Crest in order to regain the powers he lost when he was banished from Anon. He cannot ---"

"But I am to ...," she lowers her head, "I cannot complete my task if the children are hurt."

"To expose feelings is to risk exposing your true self."

"My true self?"

"To place your ideals before the eyes of others is to risk their loss."

"I have made promises."

"You must always keep your promises," Nous smiles, "promises are sacred. However, your pledge may have become fragmented in the process."

"Fragmented; of course," she looks up with a smile of relief, "I understand."

"I can offer you sanctuary at my home in the Province of Acceptance if you agree to help Anza return the Crest and the horse, and of course the others ... to their rightful place on Theia."

"You have my word," Katipo bows to Nous and moves into the cave entrance and toward Anza. She swirls her cloak around herself and becomes invisible.

Anza is scared and curled up in a corner. The Black Raccoon watches from a crevice. The Owl morphs back into the Raven as it flies in the cave perching on a high-extended ledge. They are not aware of Katipo's presence. She moves close to Anza revealing herself from under her cloak as she swirls it over Anza.

"Don't be afraid," she covers Anza's mouth to keep him from making a sound, "Nous sent me, and is waiting outside. I will take you to safety."

"I remember you. You are ---"

"We must hurry."

"They'll see us ---"

"I've got you covered."

Katipo shields Anza with her cloak as they move slowly out of the cave.

Gray Wolf looks around. "Where's the kid?"

"He's ... he was just there."

The bad guys jump up. Run around, looking in cervices, behind rocks.

"Check outside."

The Stellar Bubble Craft appears in the distant sky and descends to a point next to Anza and Katipo. Katipo steps back swirling her cloak and becomes invisible. The Craft hovers as its bright light flashes out encompassing Anza in an instant.

Katipo removes the surrounding cloak and bows to Nous with her hands together as if in prayer, Nous gestures from the Craft as it closes to its bubble form and speeds away.

Katipo stretches her arms out in front, clicks her bracelets together forming radiant circles and zooms up and away.

Gray Wolf and the bad guys run out of the cave and look around.

Gray Wolf shouts, "The horse and the girl are gone."

One of the bad guys asks, "Where did they go?"

"There's only one place. Let's get going."

Phir is standing next to his pick-up by the Qi farmhouse with the Oglala Bow in his hand as the Stellar Bubble Craft swoops in near him hovering with Nous and Anza inside. Anza steps down and rushes to Phir's side. Katipo lands nearby.

"What's she doing here?"

Anza looks up at his grandfather, "She helped me get away from Gray Wolf and the other bad guys."

Nous presents an unlikely circular thumb to first finger okay motion, "She will be helping Anza."

Anza looks around, "What happened to Q?"

"I took her home ... she is fine."

The Bubble Craft flies away with Nous. Phir raises the Bow and points it ceremonially in Nous' direction. He turns and points the Bow at Katipo with a 'don't-get-in-my-way' look on his face.

Phir takes Anza's arm and leads him to the house.

'Runs like the Wind' enters the barn and goes to his normal place, rears, sets his stance, but remains alive.

Katipo follows the horse, strokes his mane and smiles, "We'll get you home." She walks toward to the door, stretches her arms out in front, clicks her bracelets together forming the typical radiant circles and zooms up and away.

Duo adjusts the Stellar Monitor to focus on the four-dimensional planet of Anon where we see Katipo sailing through the Portal of Ojas, greeted by Nous and invited to board the Stellar Bubble Craft, which increases in size to accommodate her. They fly off on a seemingly short trip landing at the entrance to the Province of Acceptance.

Chapter Nineteen

Betrayal

We return our sights to the Stellar Monitor. Our vision focuses on Nous in the Province of Acceptance and on Earth simultaneously.

Gray Wolf and the bad guys on horseback skulk in the shadows of the old barn dismounting just as Katipo flies off.

Pointing to one of the bad guys, "Stay with the horses," Gray Wolf whispers a command and points to another, "watch the door. The rest of you come with me."

Gray Wolf and two bad guys sneak to the old barn instructing them with gestures; pointing to each of them and to different directions he wants them to go.

Still whispering, "Let's find the horse and get outta here," pointing to another bad guy, "find a halter."

One of the bad guys calls in a whisper, "Over here."

Gray Wolf joins the bad guy next to two horses.

"There're two horses that look the same. Which one do we take?"

Gray Wolf ponders the situation, "The one with a saddle. He's the one."

"Are you sure? They look the same."

The horse with the white saddle moves back and forth and rears as the bad guy grabs his reins. There is a struggle between man and horse. The saddle is loose and falls to the floor. The man wins and leads 'Runs like the Wind' to the barn door.

"Let's' go," Gray Wolf commands.

With a halter in his hand, the other bad guy asks, "what do we do with this other horse?"

"Leave him."

Gray Wolf and the bad guys silently walk away leading their horses and 'Runs like the Wind'.

* * * * * * *

Anza, lying on his bed, sees the Oracle Frame glow and hears the small 'start-the-race' trumpet sound. He sits up, rubs his eyes, puts his ring on and taps the Oracle Screen.

Xandr appears on the screen. "Hi Anza, did I wake you? "

"It's OK. What's up?"

"When are you gonna get the Crest and other stuff back here?"

"Don't know."

"February 29th is just around the corner."

"I know, I know. Yeye has the Crest, and your horse is in the old barn. Can I send Thunder instead?"

"What thunder? What are you talking about?"

"Thunder, that's his name. He's just like "Runs like the Wind'. You'd be getting a new horse and ---"

"No way. Send 'Runs like the Wind' back to me."

"Okay, okay."

"Don't forget, you gotta send that raven back too."

Meilin is calling from the kitchen, "Breakfast in five minutes."

"Ok mom."

"I gotta go ... talk later."

Anza, Phir, Baxter and Meilin are at the kitchen table finishing breakfast; Meilin is gathering the dishes.

Meilin asks, "What are you two doing today?"

"Yeye is helping me with my lessons."

"No more flying lessons; promise." Commands Baxter.

Phir ignores Baxter's comments with a smile, "Help your mother with the dishes. I'm going out to the barn."

Baxter drives off as Phir walks into the old barn and meets Katipo, who is wearing her Latrodectus outfit.

"What are you doing here?"

"Nous asked me to help."

"Where's the horse?"

"Right there," she points.

Phir inspects the horse. "This is a different horse."

"He was here last night," Katipo points to the spot where the statue normally stands.

"We have to find him and the raven. Time is drawing nigh."

"I can find the horse," Katipo says with a smirk.

Katipo takes her Transfer Ring from her pocket and places it on her finger. She touches her Abstract Data Recorder Belt Buckle and points her ring finger a few feet in front of Phir. A three-dimensional holographic image of Gray Wolf and four bad guys on horseback leading an extra horse appears. "Look. Gray Wolf has the horse," Katipo exclaims.

"How did he get ...? Change your," Phir gestures up and down toward Katipo's outfit, "and come with me."

Katipo raises her arms above her head and looks up. She sets her hands and pulls an invisible shade down to her toes. Her clothes change to a western hat, a blouse, blue jeans and boots as her hands move down to her toes.

"Do you approve?"

Phir does not answer while he leads the way into the house. He looks around, does not see Meilin and grabs Anza's arm on his way through the kitchen. They stop at the door to Anza's room.

"Get your Oracle Frame, Transfer Ring and the Medallion and meet us in the Grand Room."

When they are all together, Phir does his magic and opens the wall to the Chamber Obscura. Anza, Phir, and Katipo move in and stand at the podium. Anza is wearing his Magical Transfer Ring, and is holding the Cosmic Eye Medallion and Oracle Frame.

Katipo raises her arms above her head and looks up pulling the invisible shade down to her toes changing back to her Latrodectus outfit. She is also wearing her Magical Transfer Ring.

Phir holds the Bow upright while Anza places his ring finger on the left page of the Tome of Legends. A small rumbling sound is followed by the 'oh-oh what's happening music'.

A soft melodious voice comes from the Tome. "What do you wish, oh Chosen One?"

"I wish to speak with the Chronicle of Unchangeable Changes."

The Tome of Legends responds, "Do you wish for me to call upon the Chronicle of Unchangeable Changes?"

"Yes."

A moment passes and a voice comes from the Tome of Legends, "I am the Chronicle of Unchangeable Changes. What is your desire, oh Chosen One?"

"I need the code to transport the Crest ---"

Phir cuts him short, "Be specific Sūnzi."

"I need the code to transport the Sacred Oglala Crest, the horse, 'Runs like the Wind', the raven, Gray Wolf, and the four bad guys back to Planet Theia."

The pages of the Tome begin turning and glowing; faster and faster, brighter and brighter until music begins playing softly building to a crescendo. Suddenly, the music quiets, and the pages stop turning leaving one page aglow.

The Chronicle speaks again through the Tome, "The code you wish is encrypted on the Tome of Legends glowing page. You may cipher the code with your Cosmic Eye Medallion and transmit it to your Magical Oracle Frame. Follow the instructions that appear in the Oracle," the Chronicle pauses and its soft voice becomes a command, "be careful to use only the corresponding codes encrypted on the Sacred Oglala Crest with the cipher symbols on this page. To use other codes will be disastrous."

Anza reads the instructions with the Cosmic Eye Medallion. He turns his Oracle Frame facing the Tome of Legends. The open page of the Tome glows intensely as the entire book begins to vibrate as if it would jump-off the podium. Light rays stream out at undulating frequencies between the Tome and Oracle Frame with corresponding static discharge sounds downloading the instructions. After a few moments, the download stops and the Oracle Frame's screen fades to black.

Katipo points her belt buckle to the Tome of Legends. Another set of rays shoot from the Tome to her Abstract Data Recorder downloading the same information.

Anza looks in amazement at Katipo, "What did you just do?"

"I need the information if I'm going to help you. I'm going to find the raven and get him ready for transport."

"I think he wants something special that we can't give him. If he doesn't get it he might not go home."

Phir confirms Anza's concern, "He has to understand that Anza doesn't have the power to make those promises."

"I will take care of him. I promise."

* * * * * * *

We return our sights to the Stellar Monitor and Duo adjusts our focus on happenings in the Space-Between Dimensions. Daiyu is watching Katipo's betrayal in his Cosmos Comprehender. He begins pacing; contemplating what to do about Katipo's duplicity. He extends his huge prehistoric-like bird wings and begins flying back and forth erratically stopping at each turn with more deliberation. He flies to the outer limits of the Space-Between Dimensions. With a furious look, he throws lightning bolts toward Earth and the Qi Farm. Striking again and again shaking the ground. He is not satisfied and turns his rage toward Theia slamming the bolts at the Softwind Farm.

Anza, Phir and Katipo hear the lightning cracking sound from the safety of the Chamber Obscura.

"Daiyu has found out that I am helping you."

Anza looks at Phir, "What can we do?"

"We do not have the power to deal with Daiyu."

"Call on Nous, he will know how to deal with Daiyu," instructs Katipo.

"Yes," Phir agrees and continues, "let's go."

They hurry out to a place near the old barn.

Anza looks up calling out. "Nous ... Nous."

The Stellar Bubble Craft appears almost instantly in the dark sky and zooms down at rocket speed, slowing down and coming to rest next to Anza. Nous gets out focusing on Anza. The Craft remains hovering.

"I see that Daiyu is angry and attacking you here and Xandr on Planet Theia."

"What should we do?"

"Contact Xandr and tell him to stay in the safety of his Chamber Obscura. I will counter Daiyu's attack."

"What about our parents and ---?"

Nous interrupts, "Without the Sacred Crest, his wrath can only be directed toward you, Xandr and Katipo."

Nous turns with hands toward the sky. Intermittent Green laser-like beams propel like ground-to-air missiles from his hands towards the Space-Between-Dimensions exploding before getting to Daiyu.

"I must get closer to engage him."

Nous gets back into his Craft and rockets away.

* * * * * * *

Duo does his Portal Prompter magic and our view is redirected and ready to witness the Ultimate Battle.

The Stellar Bubble Craft approaches Daiyu in the Space-Between Dimensions. The Stellar Craft moves away and becomes invisible as Nous gets out and stands before the Black Jade.

"You come to stop me from my rightful destiny."

"You do not have the right to cause an imbalance of the planets."

"I want the Sacred Oglala Crest. You do not have control of the Crest."

"You know I am the keeper of planetary balance. The Sacred Oglala Crest must be returned to Theia along with the horse and the people or ---"

"You cannot move these people and their things. Only the Chosen One can, and he is just a boy. I am not concerned with the planets. I am very powerful, and the Crest will increase my power."

"The Space-Between-Dimensions will not exist if the planets are destroyed."

"Those little people. Ha! I will promise them riches ... they will accept ... I will rule," shouts Daiyu.

Daiyu fires a lightning bolt, then another sending Nous whirling back. Nous shakes off the attack and counters with green laser-light blasts that turn into yellow missiles from the right hand. There are more blasts from the left hand. Daiyu staggers a little, but does not falter. He responds with several weakened lightning bolts. A moment passes and both of Nous' hands are blazing green rocket-like blasts with more powerful purple missiles. The multiple missile blasts strike Daiyu propelling him away and out of sight.

Nous signals and the Stellar Bubble Craft reappears surrounding Nous, it instantly rockets away at an incredible
speed.

* * * * * * *

Duo whooshes his hand across the keypad and we are
back on Earth, materializing in the middle of an earthquake. Anza is sitting on his bed rubbing his Magical Transfer Ring with the Oracle Frame and Sacred Oglala Bow next
to him. The Oracle Frame glows emitting a small 'start-the-
race' trumpet sound. Anza picks it up and taps the screen.

An image of Xandr appears on the screen. He speaks,
"I'm scared."

"Me too, the whole place is shaking like an Earthquake."

"It's happening here too, a Theiaquake."

"Today's February 28th here. Is it the same there? "

"Yeah. One day left. What are you gonna do?"

"Me? Not just me; I've been thinking ... we-e-e ... are
going to create a diversion."

"What kind of ---"

"You and your cousins have to come here and help.
Here's what I'm thinking ..."

Anza outlines his plan. "Do you remember how to get
here?"

"Yes."

Our Earthbound Starcruiser, Totfote, materializes and
we board for our trip to the Space-Between Dimensions;
we are auto-secured in the quasi-invisible XR trans-tension
restraint system. Without a command from Solo, Duo
points to a diagram touching a series of icons in a special
sequence on the Universal Portal Prompter. There is an

instantaneous power surge and we trans-dimensionally travel arriving in a Stealth Slot at the precise time as our duplicate spacecraft and its occupants. It is a strange phenomenon to rejoin with our duplicates.

Solo instructs Duo, "Activate Earth/Theia trans audio-video."

Duo points to a diagram on the screen; he swipes an icon in our direction sending a virtual speaker to our position, and we hear voices from Theia. We watch the Stellar Monitor and see Xandr and his cousins on the Softwind Farm.

Xandr, Payta, Yellow Flower, and Little Bear, are in the middle of the stable. Xandr raises his grandfather's cane. The Waluta unfurls, and a small whirlwind surrounds them. The Cousins jump back as the Sacred Hoop appears on the floor.

"Whoa!" Payta exclaims.

"Sit inside the cangleška wakan," Xandr points, "It's a Sacred Hoop. It's where we'll connect to Anza's world.

"Connect? Wha'dya mean?" Asks Little Bear, "he's gonna come here isn't he?"

"I'm thinking that it's not gonna be that way. Huh?" exclaims Payta.

Yellow Flower looks puzzled, "Are we going there?"

"Don't worry," Xandr assures them, "we'll be safe."

"You ever do this before?" Little Bear squirms.

Payta looks at Xandr, "I betcha ---"

Xandr takes charge. "Let's get started."

Xandr, Payta, Yellow Flower, and Little Bear, are sitting within the Sacred Hoop. A chill moves through the Softwind stable. The cousins watch silently as Xandr lifts the Waluta Vision Quest Cane high up. He closes his eyes tilting his head back; he sings an ancient Lakota time travel chant. The Waluta begins waving in the tranquil space; slowly at first, then fluttering as if a strong wind was blowing, but there was none.

The filtered moonlight through the cracks in the stable walls and roof soon dissipates leaving a pitch dark 'quiet-before-the-storm' eerie feeling; moments seem like a lifetime until a great vibration followed by a thunderous clap shudders the old building that feels like it should crumble and fall. Suddenly the darkness becomes a soft glow, which rapidly intensifies to a lightening bright illumination, filling the room accompanied by a small breeze that quickly turns into a force whisking them up and out the doorway.

Chapter Twenty

The Diversion

In the Stellar Monitor, we see Xandr and his cousins trans-traveling from the Softwind Farm stable on Planet Theia materializing in the center of the old barn on the Qi Farm on Earth.

Anza, Qingling, Arthur, and Longwei stand in awe.

Katipo walks in wearing her Latrodectus outfit. She looks around. "We're all here. Good. It's getting dark. It's time to get to work."

"Who are you?" Asks the wide-eyed thirteen-year-old Payta as he stares at the shapely Katipo with a curious smile.

"Never mind," Anza assures Xandr's cousin, "she's here to help. Nous said it's okay."

"So-o-o ... what's next." Xandr looks at Anza.

"First ... first of all we gotta get together."

Anza lifts the Bow high up. The deer's tail waves and creates a great vibration and a thunderous clap. All the kids tremble as a circle of stones appears on the floor.

Anza motions with the Bow, "Everybody inside the circle."

"I'll be right back." Katipo turns and leaves.

Longwei looks in wonderment, "Is this gonna turn into a rocket ship, and ---?"

Anza cuts in; "No rockets Longster. Don't let your imagination get ahead of us. Here's the plan." Anza outlines how they are going to create a distraction and how he will send everything back to Theia.

Katipo appears in front of the Sheng Chi Master who is walking on the dirt road. She faces him and bows with her hands together as if in prayer.

"Mighty Sheng Chi Master," she pauses for a moment then lifting her head, she notices an old Indian standing behind the Master. "Who is---?"

"He is Running Bear, a great Lakota medicine man; and my counterpart from Planet Theia. He followed Black Elk and his scoundrels. He is here to help with the transference if he is needed."

"I am here to help Anza. I must find the raven," Katipo announces.

"I am pleased you have decided to use your powers to assist the Chosen One," he pauses for a moment and puts his hands together turning the palms facing up.

Running Bear takes a Sacred Red Stone Pipe from under his buckskin robe and moves to the right side of the Sheng Chi Master lighting the pipe. "Because you are of Chinese and Lakota ancestry, we will administer a combined blessing to accelerate your efforts."

Katipo reverently receives a glowing Tao blessing from the Sheng Chi Master and a 'Visible Breath' sent to the Great Spirit from the Lakota Medicine Man's pipe.

The Sheng Chi Master continues, "The raven is with Gray Wolf. He has taken the shape of an owl and is perched in the Sugi tree watching for the right time to steal the Crest."

Katipo is adamant, "You must go to a place out of harm's way. I am helping Anza, and will be leaving Planet Earth soon. I will be taking everything that belongs on the Planet Theia."

"We will be by the Old Mill if you need us."

"Running Bear must be included in the transference."

"He will be there when the time is right."

"Be safe."

Katipo bows in reverence to the Sheng Chi Master and Lakota Medicine Man. She turns, stretching her arms out in front of her clicking her bracelets together. An energy field appears broadcasting radiant circles. She raises her arms to the sky and zooms up and away.

"She has great powers," proclaims Running Bear.

"It is good that she has given up her allegiance with the Black Jade to help the Chosen One."

The Sheng Chi Master and the Medicine Man turn away and walk to the Old Mill.

Katipo circles slowly descending to a graceful landing near the Sugi tree where Gray Wolf, Nigel Churchill, Black Elk and the other bad guys are holed up. She surveys the situation seeing their horses across the road in the meadow, the Owl perched in the tree and the Black Raccoon hiding behind the tree. She walks with determination toward the tree, stopping directly in front of Gray Wolf.

One of the bad guys points. "Look at the pretty girl."

Gray Wolf bellows a hardy laugh. "Look at what we have here; the space-between girl." He inspects her and continues, "Looking for the horse?"

"My Name is Katipo Magicaln, and I know where the horse is. But, you must ---"

"Must what?" shouts the smug Gray Wolf, "you gonna make us do something?"

Katipo stretches her arms out in front of Gray Wolf and his cohorts clicking her bracelets together and opening her arms as if she were embracing the space around them. An energy field forms broadcasting radiant multi-colored circles hanging above the men and their horses in the meadow. The radiant circles imprison them as she lowers her arms. The men struggle and the horses try to run, but are captured in the energy circles. Katipo looks austere at the men sending them and their mounts sailing away bouncing around in the northern sky.

The smiling Katipo turns to the Owl. "I know you are Dimitri in a different form. It's your turn. Bring the horse, 'Runs like the Wind', here and I will grant your wish. Do not and I will do the same to you." She looks at the black raccoon behind the tree, "Leave or I'll turn you into a prickly plant."

The raccoon scurries off to the old barn.

The Owl morphs into a shaking raven and submits to her offer. "I want my own plantation on Theia with a stable of thoroughbred horses and many slaves. I want more money than I could ever spend and a beautiful wife."

"I remember, and your wish will be granted upon the arrival of these," ... she points to her captives in the sky, "and the horse and saddle with the Sacred Oglala Crest, and of course, you will be Dimitri Talbot once again."

Katipo glances away from the bird, but with a quick turn back she instructs, "You must bring the horse to me tonight. You do know where he is?"

"I don't think I can get the horse. Nigel had him taken away and Carl Drinkwater is keeping him in a corral out on the North Forty. I can get the saddle from the old barn, but I don't have the Crest anymore."

"Do not worry about the Crest. Bring the saddle to me. Anza must know where the corral and this North Forty are located."

* * * * * * *

Anza, Qingling, Arthur, Longwei, Xandr, Little Bear, Payta, and Yellow Flower are in the old barn standing in the Circle of Stones. The Black Raccoon scampers into a dark corner and watches from behind a hay bale.

Katipo returns exclaiming, "I have Gray Wolf, and the others from Theia secured where they won't get in the way. The raven will bring me the saddle ... but," she looks at Anza and Xandr, "you have to get the horse."

Xandr asks, "Okay, so where is he?"

Looking at Anza, "The raven said he is in a place called the North Forty."

"That's way out at the far end of our property."

"How long will it take to get there?"

"It's a long way out there. It'll probably take the better part of a day; and then all night to get back here."

Xandr looks at Anza. "We're running out of time. You're gonna have to do some extreme magic, oh-h-h Chosen One."

"We're all going. Do you remember the diversion we discussed? It's time. Everyone outside," he looks at Xandr, "except you," he grabs Xandr's arm. "We'll be right back."

Anza and Xandr run out of the barn and into the house. They continue through the kitchen and grand room stopping only for the normal incantation before entering the Chamber Obscura.

Anza with his Magical Transfer Ring, Cosmic Eye Medallion and Oracle Frame; Xandr with his Magical Transfer Ring and Picture Frame go directly to the podium. The Oglala Bow and Waluta Cane are propped against the podium.

Xandr looks around, "Where's the Crest?"

"Yeye put it in here." Anza puts his hand into the barely discernible place in the podium. "Ahh; here it is. Now we're ready."

"Wha'dya mean? Ready?"

"We are going to transport you, me and the Cuz to the North Forty," he smiles an iniquitous smile, "come on."

Chapter Twenty-one

Daiyu's Retaliation

We return our sights to the Stellar Monitor and the Space-Between Dimensions as Daiyu recovers from his encounter with Nous. He furiously searches the Cosmos Comprehender. He starts tapping the screen; it changes to various images. This is not what he wants; frustrated, he finally locates Katipo going into the barn. Searching the length and breadth of the Qi Farm, he finally detects the captured Gray Wolf and his cohorts floating in the sky wrapped in energy circles.

With a space-shattering howl, Daiyu readies himself. He starts throwing lightning bolts toward the Earth Planet.

Moments later Duo points to a diagram on the screen touching a series of icons bringing us to the point of the blasts. We hear and see the lightning bolts as they find their target blasting the circles around Gray Wolf and the other ban guys setting them free.

Gray Wolf and the gang fall to the ground a short distance from the North Forty. They pick themselves up and ramble around in astonishment. Their horses land in a nearby meadow.

"I don't know where that came from," Gray Wolf hollers, "but we gotta git." They run to the meadow and round-up their horses. "Mount up."

Gray Wolf and his gang ride away down the dirt road toward the North Forty.

Qingling, Arthur, Longwei, Little Bear, Payta and Yellow Flower are standing by the door just outside of the old barn as the lightning bolts find their targets. Katipo comes out from the doorway looking to the sky.

Anza and Xandr rush from the house to join with the others.

Qingling, in a frightened voice, "What was that sound?"

Katipo sheds some light, "It must be Daiyu; it sounds like he's shooting lightning bolts again."

The ever-inquisitive Longwei echoes, "Shooting lightning bolts?"

"Yes, he throws a tantrum by hurling lightning bolts through space when he doesn't get his way."

Mister inquisitive continues, "What does he do when he's really mad?"

"You don't want to know."

Katipo sets her ring, pointing out in front of the kids, and a three-dimensional holographic image of Gray Wolf and bad guys on horseback appears. "This is not good. They are somewhere in the distance going away from here. Do they know where 'Runs like the Wind' is?"

Longwei looks at the holographic image, "They're heading out to the North Forty."

Katipo sees the black raccoon peering from inside the barn door. She clicks her bracelets together and points her ring finger with a sinister smirk. The raccoon morphs into a prickly bush and bounces around.

* * * * * * *

Duo adjusts the Stellar Monitor and we are directed to the four-dimensional world where Anon is watching the Cosmos Comprehender with great concern.

The Grey Forms move to face him.

"It is time for the Thunder Beings. Send them to meet with Nous. Have them positioned and ready to assist the Chosen One. He will be calling soon. They will know what to do."

The Grey Forms bow to the Immortal Unknown and de-materialize.

Chapter Twenty-two
Thunder Beings

Duo is busy resetting the Stellar Monitor as the scenes begin to change rapidly with the happenings. This time it is back to Earth where Anza is facing Qingling, Arthur, Long-wei, Xandr, Little Bear, Payta, Yellow Flower and Katipo, who are standing by the door to the old barn.

"Ready?"

There are silent and cautious nods from everyone.

Anza is holding the Bow while Xandr has the Waluta Cane readied. Anza tugs Xandr's arm pulling him close. He motions for the others to move in and stand close together.

The cousins gather in the Circle of Stones with anxiety, anticipation and a lot of fear of the unknown.

Anza looks at Xandr with a demanding face, "Ready."

Xandr nods with some trepidation, "Ready."

Anza and Xandr raise the Bow and Cane up to the sky and watch as a small bright cloud appears.

"Thunder Beings ... Thunder Beings," Anza shouts.

Thunderous sounds and lighting flashes rise up filling the sky. Then, without warning, the Thunder Beings' booming voices come from nowhere and everywhere at once. "Go, Chosen One. Go to the far reaches of your land and discover the horse, 'Runs like the Wind'. We will await you there."

The cloud changes to green, then blue, then lavender and speeds away vanishing into the northern sky.

Little Bear shouts in astonishment, "Thunder Beings, I've heard of them, but never ... wow!"

"Everyone get ready, here we go." Anza calls out in Chinese, 'raise us high ... transport with my thoughts', "Tígao women gao ... Jiaotong yu ow de xiangfa."

Anza, Xandr, their cousins and Katipo transform into semi-fluid forms encased in a cloud-like substance and rise slowly, increasing their speed faster and faster until they zoom off into the sky toward the North Forty.

The kids and Katipo slow down landing softly behind a rock outcropping as the cloud dissipates and they return too their normal forms. The corral is just a few yards away.

Qingling points, "There, look ... there's the horse."

'Runs like the Wind' is standing by a small tack shed.

There are hoof beats in the distance with dust rising on the dirt road as Gray Wolf and his gang race toward the corral.

Xandr shouts to the others in a voice just above a whisper. "Duck down!"

Anza looks for the Thunder Beings, but does not see them. "Nous ... Nous."

Nous appears in an instant and hovers a short distance behind the rocks in the Stellar Bubble Craft. "Anza. Your plan to have everyone run toward the corral, making noise and create a diversion is good. Remember to open the gate and have everyone go inside the corral. Tell Xandr to mount his horse, and ride it around inside the corral so Gray Wolf and the bad guys will try to capture the horse.

Close the gate when everyone is inside the corral. Summon the Thunder Beings. I will see you later."

"Where are you going?"

"I have some unfinished business."

The Stellar Bubble Craft speeds away.

Anza waves at the kids, "Follow me ... make a lot of noise," turning to Xandr, "get your horse and trot him around inside the corral."

The kids run and holler. Anza opens the gate with a come-on gesture for the kids to run inside the corral.

Xandr motions and the horse bows down on one knee as he steps on a horizontal fence rail and swings on the bareback steed. Grabbing the mane, he shouts, "Come on, hiyah, hiyah." 'Runs like the Wind' responds with an instant gait like a thoroughbred manège.

Gray Wolf and his gang ride into the corral thinking they have the upper hand. Suddenly, Gray Wolf becomes suspicious of the surroundings. He dismounts and grabs a handful of dirt throwing it in the air. He looks to the ground and shouts, "Iwakta ye Howiwacipi."

Dirt colored ghostly forms rise from the ground flying in an erratic manner in and out and through the unsuspecting kids. The Ghost Dancers start growling and gnashing at everything in sight, and immediately, they target Anza's Sacred Oglala Bow and Xandr's Waluta Cane. Anza directs his Magical Transfer Ring laser at them creating a temporary distraction.

Gray Wolf redirects the Ghost Dancers to concentrate their attack on Xandr and his horse. They surround them gnashing with the vigor of a frightening enemy. 'Runs like the Wind' rears with his forelegs fighting off the aggressors as Xandr struggles to stay aboard.

Realizing the danger to Xandr, Anza runs and closes the gate. He raises his arms and points the Sacred Oglala Bow upward to the sky calling the 'Thunder Beings' in Chinese. "Léi zhòngsheng ... Léi zhòngsheng."

A small bright cloud appears with the sounds of thunder and cracking lighting flashing through the sky. The lightning bolts target the ghostly images in the corral. The Ghost Dancers are no match to the powerful Thunder Beings, and splatter into dust clouds, and are absorbed by the Thunder Beings' flashes and whisked away into outer space.

The Thunder Beings are back on track and the crackling lightning resumes in a circular pattern forcing everyone inside a circle of energy.

A booming surreal voice comes from nowhere and everywhere at once "take them away," as Gray Wolf and his band of scoundrels cower in fear.

Anza jumps into the circle and raises his Bow, pointing it to everyone in the corral then to the sky. He surveys the situation, and raises the Sacred Oglala Bow up to the multi-colored sky and chants in Chinese 'raise us high, transport with my thoughts', "Tígao women gao, Jiaotong yu ow de xiangfa."

All the kids, 'Runs like the Wind', Katipo, Gray Wolf and the bad guys on their horses rise slowly at first, then faster as they zoom off into the sky. The Thunder Beings' cloud changes to green, then blue, then lavender and speeds away vanishing into the sky.

Chapter Twenty-three
The Final Conflict

Solo is studying the Stellar Monitor, looks up at Duo and says, "Something is about to happen with Daiyu."

Without any further instructions, Duo points to a diagram on the screen touching a multitude of icons and we rocket to the Space-Between Dimensions. We hear voices from the Space-Between Dimensions as Daiyu appears watching us in the Comprehender. The Stellar Bubble Craft approaches from another direction.

Solo instructs, "Move to the safety of a stealth slot." Duo responds and we slide into the slot.

Daiyu turns away from us and directs his attention to Nous' Stellar Bubble Craft. He hurls numerous lightning charges, but the Craft avoids the assault by zigzagging and finally engaging its Averteron shield.

The Averteron shield weakens from the constant lightening blasts. Nous activates a cloaking device and moves forward to an attack position. The stealth Bubble Craft fires beams at Daiyu's position knocking out his Comprehender. The Craft settles in behind Daiyu.

Nous approaches Daiyu from the rear. "Looking for me?"

"I have been waiting for this moment."

"You have become more determined to rule the planets without any regard for the inhabitants."

"I have become more powerful."

"More evil since being banned from the Fourth Dimension does not make you powerful. Your evil and power are not in balance." Nous continues and positions for the impending battle. Suddenly, Nous' childlike voice changes to a strong authoritarian declaration with a roar, "I AM THE BALANCE."

Daiyu whirls around into an offensive position. The two are motionless ... waiting ... waiting. The Black Jade spreads his wings and lunges forward with uncanny speed. He throws several lightning bolts.

Nous skillfully blocks the bolts with his laser beams. Motionless again, they wait. The Black Jade extends his enormous wings again and readies for the kill.

Daiyu and Nous engage in their mighty battle. A time without beginning or end continues. Daiyu flies over Nous shooting lightning bolts. Nous dodges, launching a counter attack of laser beams while maneuvering the Craft. Numerous laser volleys weaken Daiyu's attack.

Finally, aware of his opponent's condition, Nous disengages the stealth protector and rises out of the Stellar Bubble Craft to meet his opponent head on with determined eyes fixed. Nous blasts lasers from both hands at a distance that is only a breath away.

Daiyu responds with a weakened volley of lightning bolts that Nous easily diverts.

Once again, Nous blasts with both hands, but this time with maximum strength lasers that rock the very depths of Daiyu as he plunges uncontrollably, twisting and turning in an endless pandemonium. A final barrage from Nous sends Daiyu into space in a shower of brilliant light that turns dark red. Daiyu vanishes into the pits of a red light that becomes a globe bouncing around in the depths of outer space.

Chapter Twenty-four

Balance

Solo is studying the Stellar Monitor, looks up at Duo and says, "It's time to return to Planet Earth for the transition."

Without any further instructions, Duo points to a diagram on the monitor touching a multitude of icons and we rocket to Earth.

Everyone inside the Thunder Beings' energy circle lands in the corral near the old barn on the Qi Farm as directed by Anza. Katipo jumps away stretching her arms out clicking her bracelets together creating a new energy field, which broadcasts radiant circles. The radiant circles hover above everyone, imprisoning them as she lowers her arms.

"Hey! Remember us?" Cries Xandr.

Katipo smiles a new kind of smile, almost as a mother has for her children. "You must remain for the trip, but the other children will stay here" She turns to the Earth based children and points her ring. One-by-one Katipo raises Anza, Qingling, Arthur and Longwei up-and-out of the radiant circles and down to safety next to the corral.

"I gotta learn how to do that," shouts Anza.

The Raven flies over and perches atop the corral fence.

Katipo motions, "Come Dimitri, bring the saddle and you will receive your reward."

The Raven morphs into a stronger Owl and flies into the old barn returning with the saddle in its talons.

Katipo, using her Transfer Ring, captures the Owl, and slowly lowers him into the confinement of Radiant Circles. The Owl morphs back into the Raven.

She moves and secures the white saddle to 'Runs like the Wind'; she raises Xandr up and places him on 'Runs like the Wind's saddle.

"Are we ready to transfer?" asks Anza.

"Not yet." Katipo looks around and sees Running Bear walking toward the corral with the Sheng Chi Master. She goes to meet them. Bowing in reverence to the Sheng Chi Master, she turns to Running Bear, "the time has come," she links her arm to his and escorts him to the corral.

The Medicine Man gives her a warm hug, raises his bow and sails into the confines of the Circles.

"Now," shouts Katipo as she looks to Anza.

Phir walks toward Anza. "It's your turn."

"Yeye ... everything is ready."

"I have the crest here," Phir reaches in his pocket.

Anza takes the Sacred Oglala Crest from his grandfather. He looks down, and studies the markings on the Crest, "Time to go home." With a motion as if skipping a stone across a lake, he zaps it into place on the white saddle as a volley of brilliant sparks fly from the saddle as it sighs. Anza looks at Katipo, turns his attention to Phir, and finally looks at all those secured in the Radiant Circles making sure nothing is missing.

"What if they don't go where they're s'posed to go?"

"You studied the word. The children will go home; the Thunder Beings will take charge of Gray Wolf and his gang back on Theia," he pauses looking at Katipo, "and Katipo has arranged for the raven's reward after its return. I have talked to the Sheriff about Nigel. It's time."

Anza stands facing the Radiant Circles' captives. He reaches into his pocket and removes a silver necklace he took from the silver box moments ago, and attaches it to the Cosmic Eye Medallion placing it around his neck.

Katipo nods approval.

Pointing his Magical Transfer Ring Anza raises the Bow, leans his head back, chants in Chinese, 'gather all the people and objects', "Shoují suoyou de rén hé wùti." He waits and looks around at the good and bad captives.

Gray Wolf and the bad guys struggle to escape. Xandr sits apprehensively on 'Runs like the Wind' and his cousins move around as they wait impatiently.

Anza readies himself for the final moment, looks to the sky and chants another command,
"Fhuí dào tamen de xingqiú."

A powerful golden beam shines down from the sky as he turns the bow sideways for its full force. The beam widens into a massive inverted cone until it encompasses the sky directly above those within the Radiant Circles.

A laser-like beam streams from Anza's ring toward the sky as he leans back a little more repeating the final command, "Fanhuí dào tamen de xingqiú." The golden beam of light from the sky unites with the beam from the Sacred Oglala Bow with a thunderous blast that quiets to a heavenly melody.

The stars disappear as the sky changes colors from black to blue to red then yellow and finally becomes an eerie shade of green. The inverted cone changes into a swirling funnel and zooms down inside the limits of the Radiant Circles. The swirling stops for a brief moment until all things in the Radiant Circles begin to lift off the ground into the inverted tornado-like funnel rotating slowly at first picking up speed as it rockets into the changing sky.

There is a warm, calming silence as the sky changes through a myriad of colors finally returning to its natural state as Anza, Phir, Katipo and the cousins watch the return of balance to the universe.

Katipo breaks the silence, "I must go."

* * * * * * *

Solo strikes a pad at the command center. Solo Instructs, "Let's go."

Duo's hands flash across the futuristic keypad and our spacecraft transforms into a transparent cylinder, "fold space-time."

Suddenly with an unusual ease the Portal expands sucking us into it; we are auto-secured in the quasi-invisible XR trans-tension restraint system; we travel through a space-time continuum arriving at the outskirts of the four-dimensional world of Anon. Our combined starship hovers above in a stealth slot as we observe a bizarre happening.

Katipo welcomes Dimitri mounted on a thoroughbred horse on a mid-west farm that looks like an old Southern Plantation on Planet Theia. He dismounts and they go inside an elegant home. They walk through the mansion to a room filled with gold and jewels where he welcomes a beautiful and loving woman to his side. Dimitri smiles and bows like an elegant southern gentleman.

The images zoom out. Katipo leaves the scene, which is in a gilded picture frame on the stable wall. Dimitri lives in a make-believe world inside the picture frame.

Katipo flies out of the picture frame joining Nous and Anza at the Cosmos Comprehender in the Province of Acceptance on the four-dimensional world of Anon.

They are watching Nicholas Gray Wolf, Black Elk and the other bad guys sitting with their hands and feet bound inside a large ceremonial Tipi in front of a Lakota Tribal Council. The members of the Council pass the Sacred Pipe as they contemplate the penalty.

The Chief looks up with the complexity of the final authority presenting the pipe in our direction as if he knew we were watching.

The view on the screen changes to Running Bear stopping to look back before entering his Tipi.

Anza activates his Magical Oracle Fame. Nous nods approval. An image of Xandr and his cousins appears.

"I just wanted to see if you got home okay."

Xandr is sitting on 'Runs like the Wind', "Yeah we did," as he strokes his horse.

Payta standing next to the horse with the other kids shouts, "What a trip."

"Until next time," Anza closes the Oracle Frame.

* * * * * * *

Nous smiles, "I saved this for last, watch."

A calendar appears on the Cosmos Comprehender. Pages turn back and forth in a searching frenzy, suddenly stopping at FEBRUARY 30TH. The page vibrates in a counterclockwise motion, becoming progressively larger and larger evolving into a Hurricane Black Hole. Off in deep space we see a struggling Daiyu captured in a Red Transparent Globe. The globe flies to the calendar and is sucked into the Black Hole with an ear-shattering thunderclap.

The calendar closes with a title, THE CALENDAR OF LOST DAYS. The calendar moves away diminishing to the never-ending center point of our perspective.

Our Portal Prompter expands to display Anza traveling to Earth and simultaneously presenting a pleased vision of the Immortal Unknown.

Nous watches Anza in the Comprehender as he trans-travels back to Earth landing on the Qi farm near his new horse Thunder.

Anza mounts Thunder and looks around with a satisfied grin. Thunder rears and they race down the road.

Nous smiles, "Go now Little Chosen One. Destiny will call again."

Chíota

Epilogue

Solo sends a request to reverse the RSR. The Stellar Monitor flashes a message, 'Prepare to convert'.

Duo manipulates a series of icons and a new expanding diagram on the Monitor. The conversion begins with a reversal of our replication.

We find ourselves inside the Intermix Chamber, once again swallowed up by a Helicase, which rewinds the strands around us separating our mirrored duplicate DNA proteins into individual segments.

We look around and find ourselves divided from our duplicates while being whisked away to the farthest reaches of the Chamber. A fractured opening appears in the Nebula and we find ourselves sailing above the crystallized path. A mysterious force captures us, and instantly transports us the length of the path. We look back to the silver cloud-like Replication Synchronization Nebula and see our duplicates disappear into outer space.

We have a cosmic feeling we will rejoin our replicas in the not to distant future when we start our search for the calendar of lost days.

Glossary

Aberration:
> A departure from the normal or typical

Abstract Data Recorder:
> A device in Katipo's belt buckle that can upload and download an unlimited amount of data

Algorithmic string pattern:
> Pattern matching format using algorithms that do not require any processing

Algorithmic:
> A set of rules for solving a problem in a finite number of steps

Apparition:
> A ghostly appearance of a person or thing

Axis Mundi:
> World tree (center of the world)

Cangleška Wakan:
> Sacred Hoop

Center of Consciousness:
> The Universal Creator

Chamber Obscura:
> A magical place and home to the Tome of Legends on Earth and the Chronicle of Unchangeable Changes on Theia

Chanunpa Wakan:
> Sacred Pipe

Chíota:
> Chinese-Lakota Hybrid - More to come (Chíxù+Ota = Chíota)

Chota Invisibility Cloak:
> Katipo's Cloak that renders her invisible

Conscientiousness of the Ages:

        An accumulation of specific social traits

Coronal Loop:

        Energy of many different wavelengths in the
        outermost layer of the Sun's atmosphere

Cosmos Comprehender:

        A super Universal Computer that can access data
        from the entire universe

Enneagon:

        A nine-sided polygon; a nonagon

Epicene:

        Lacking any gender distinction

Ethereal:

        Seeming to belong to another world

Ethereal Cortex:

        A never-ending heavenly world

Etoftot:

        The duplicate mirror image of Totfote

Helicase:

        A place that unwinds DNA

Hyperdrive:

        Traveling faster the speed of light

Hyper-Trans:

        Super high-speed laser beams

Interloper:

        A person who becomes involved in a place where
        they are considered not to belong

Intermix Chamber:

        A space within the Pearl Pavilion used for   Replication Synchronization Ritual (RSR)

Interstitial:

        A space between other spaces

Kakapi:

        Lakota for Statue

Katipo Magicaln:
> Katipo's full name

Kelvin:
> A temperature scale used for outer space whose zero degree = -273.15°C and -459.67°F

Latrodectus:
> The katipo, an endangered spider common only to New Zealand and the transformed version in the Space-Between Dimensions

Multi-striated:
> Alternating stripes

Ordering Force:
> The Creator of the Universe

Paesre:
> The past, present and future combined

Path of Knowledge:
> The place where the Chosen One goes to learn and understand ancient mysteries

Pearl Pavilion:
> The ultimate place for RSR

Pentagonal strands:
> Five sided strands used in DNA replication

Platinum Chota Transport Bracelets:
> Katipo's Magical Bracelets

Portal of Ojas:
> Entry to the Essential Energy of the Body and the Fluid of Life; connects the mind to the body and consciousness.

Province of Acceptance:
> Nous' home in the four-dimensional world

Quantum Teleportation:
> A process to transmit objects from one location to a different location faster than the speed of light

Replication Synchronization Nebula:
> The ultimate place for RSR

Replication Synchronization Ritual (RSR):

> The process of duplicating DNA for synchronistic occupation of duplicate planets

Rigui:

> A timepiece dial

Sacred Calf Pipe:

> Lists seven rites given by White Buffalo Calf Woman for proper living and embraces all Spirits as One Spirit, and all Powers as One Power

Sacred Oglala Bow:

> An instrument of Thunder Being magic as passed down by the original medicine man Black Road

Sacred Oglala Crest:

> A Magnifying Cipher Glass

Solar Wind:

> A stream of charged particles released from the upper atmosphere of the Sun in all directions at speeds of about 400 km/s (about 1 million mph)

Stealth Averteron:

> An invisible shield that diverts attacks

Stealth Chota Cloak:

> An invisibility cloak

Stealth Slot:

> A safe harbor for a Spacecraft

Stealth Slot Mode:

> Unique data needed to enter a Stealth Slot

Stellar Monitor:

> Double-sided transparent display with unlimited touch interaction

Sugi Tree:

> Sacred Chinese Cedar

Supplication:

> To humbly ask for or plead for something

Synchro Gateway:

> The entrance to the Residence of the Most High

Synchronistic:
> Simultaneous ... at the same time

Tack shed:
> A place to store saddles, bridles, stirrups, etc.

The Presence:
> The Creator, the Highest Power

Ťhakóža:
> Grandson in Lakota

Tian yì:
> Chosen One (Chinese)

Space-Time Continuum:
> A four-dimensional mathematical model that combines space and time into a single idea

Trans-Audio:
> Quantum Interstellar communication

Trans-conversion:
> Seeming to belong to another world

Trans-Dimensional Travel:
> A method of traveling at the will of the traveler

Tribal Waluta:
> A long, narrow red prayer flag

Ultimate Duration:
> Forever ... Infinity ... without limit

Universal Portal Prompter:
> Quantum flow of unlimited information

Vision Quest Cane:
> Lakota Ceremonial Instrument

Wakatanka, Aye:
> Great Spirit

Way Station:
> A place between stations on a route

Witko tkoke wija pi:
> Crazy Woman

Yuto keca:
> Change (to)